"Attending that party was unavoidable, Rachel."

A bitter laugh left her throat. "As well as my having to fend off countless snide remarks, I suppose? I should call a press conference of my own along the lines of 'My husband, the sex symbol.'"

"You know damned well that ninety percent of gossip is conjecture."

"I need only concern myself with a paltry ten percent then!"

"Rachel!" Laz warned. "If I did a fraction of the things my publicity suggests..."

But she was too caught up in her hurt and anger to heed him. "I should never have let you coerce me into coming back here." She rounded on him in fury. "I'm going to bed—and not *yours*!"

"The hell you're not!"

Books by Helen Bianchin

HARLEQUIN PRESENTS

HARLEQUIN ROMANCE

These books may be available at your local bookseller.

Don't miss any of our special offers. Write to us at the following address for information on our newest releases.

Harlequin Reader Service
P.O. Box 52040, Phoenix, AZ 85072-2040
Canadian address: P.O. Box 2800, Postal Station A,
5170 Yonge St., Willowdale, Ont. M2N 6J3

HELEN BIANCHIN

bitter encore

Harlequin Books

TORONTO • NEW YORK • LONDON
AMSTERDAM • PARIS • SYDNEY • HAMBURG
STOCKHOLM • ATHENS • TOKYO • MILAN

Harlequin Presents first edition December 1985
ISBN 0-373-10839-7

Original hardcover edition published in 1985
by Mills & Boon Limited

CHAPTER ONE

IT was well after ten when Rachel unlocked her car and slipped behind the wheel. With a deft flick of her wrist she fired the ignition, reversed out of her space in the car-park building, then eased the Porsche Targa down to street level.

She felt tired, more so than usual—no doubt due to the fact she'd instructed all three aerobic dance classes for the studio, instead of her usual two. A faint sigh left her lips as she urged the sports car into the stream of city traffic. Thank heavens she started a week's vacation tomorrow!

Brisbane after dark held a magical quality, bright neon lights providing colourful movement as they flashed advertising slogans and vied for attention with their competitors.

The house she shared with Millie in suburban St Lucia took anything from ten to twenty minutes to reach, depending on the density of traffic. Tonight she made it in fifteen, and she slid the car into the garage, switched off the engine, then locked up and made her way indoors.

The lights were still on, and as she entered the lounge Millie looked up for a fraction of a second in mute acknowledgment of her presence before allowing the television screen to reclaim her rapt attention.

Rachel made straight for the bedroom, stripped off her tracksuit and leotard, caught up a nightshirt and towelling robe, then she crossed to the bathroom and turned on the shower.

Slowly the weariness began to leave her body, and she lingered, luxuriating beneath the warm cascading water before emerging to towel herself dry. Her toilette completed, she shrugged into the robe and made her way to the kitchen.

Minutes later she switched off the whistling kettle, poured boiling water over instant coffee, added artificial sweetener, then carried the mug to the lounge and sank into a comfortable chair.

'Tough day?' Millie queried sympathetically, and Rachel summoned a wry grimace.

'No worse than usual.' A rueful smile widened her generous mouth. 'Exuding vitality and unlimited energy tends to become a bit wearying after a while.'

'Any objection to getting away early tomorrow?'

Rachel closed her eyes in self-defence against the other girl's enthusiasm. 'Millie, have a heart,' she protested. 'I had hoped to sleep in.'

'You can sleep all you want tomorrow—on the beach,' Millie responded firmly, her bright eyes positively sparkling. 'All that golden sand and rolling surf. I can't wait.'

She gave an audible groan, then took a reviving sip of coffee. 'There's no chance of persuading you to change your mind, I suppose?'

'Not a hope,' the other girl grinned irrepressibly. 'I'm all packed. I'll even be magnanimous and offer to help you with yours.'

'Did anyone ever tell you you're impossible?'

'Countless times. It's half my attraction.' Her elfin features split into a puckish smile. 'It makes up for my lack of beauty.'

'There's nothing wrong with you,' Rachel defended, and Millie wrinkled her nose in self-deprecation.

'When you're around, I can't begin to compete.'

Her eyes narrowed fractionally, and Millie rushed kindly——

'Oh, don't look like that. You're so darned *nice*, despite the way you look, that I absolutely love you to death. There's not a single thing I can find to dislike. Oh hell,' she groaned helplessly. 'I'm making a mess of it, as usual.'

'I believe you've just paid me a backhanded compliment—at least, I think you have,' Rachel amended musingly, and Millie burst into laughter.

'I *have*—sincerely, believe me.'

'Thank you,' she responded solemnly. 'So—what time do you call *early*?'

'Seven?'

'You're joking.'

'Well, eight, then. Come on, Rachel,' Millie beseeched. 'One week in the classiest apartment block on Queensland's coastal strip. I want to *get* there, and enjoy living in the lap of unmitigated luxury.' She leaned forward in her chair. 'Come on, into the bedroom with you. I'll drag out your suitcase, and you can sit on the bed and simply say *yes* or *no* to everything I pull out of your wardrobe. You really won't have to do a thing.'

It was far easier to comply, Rachel decided with resignation as she watched Millie extract one garment after another and hold them out for approval.

'You've got beautiful luggage,' Millie murmured enviously as she chose a compact piece from the set of three and placed it on top of the bed.

'Thank you.' Monogrammed *Vuitton*, a legacy from those quixotic days when common sense had been overruled by wild rapturous passion. A faintly hysterical laugh bubbled in her throat as she caught sight of the gold-plated letters on her suitcase. She hadn't even had to change the initials. 'Okay, that's it, I think.' Millie cast a critical eye over the heap of clothes strewn across the bed.

'We're only going for a week,' Rachel alluded a trifle wryly. 'I don't need half of those. Two bikinis, a couple of sunfrocks, a few skirts and blouses, plus underwear, were all I intended taking.'

'Better to have too many and not need them, than not enough,' the other girl declared prosaically as she transferred everything with the utmost efficiency. 'There,' she murmured with satisfaction. 'That only leaves make-up and toiletries for the morning.'

She was a sweet girl, kindhearted and utterly sincere. What's more, she didn't pry. Rachel slid off the bed and stretched her arms high above her head. 'Thanks,' she accorded gently. 'You're an angel.'

'I know,' Millie acknowledged with an impudent grin. 'One day some man is going to discover my virtues and sweep me off my feet.' She spared her watch a quick glance and gave an audible groan. 'Today just became yesterday. I'm going to bed, otherwise we'll never get away before lunch.'

They left shortly after nine, slipping into the stream of south-bound traffic *en route* to the Pacific Highway, the racy yellow Porsche eating up the kilometres with ease.

Rachel had visited Surfer's Paradise several times during the past two years, yet not once did she fail to experience a spiritual lift on sighting the sparkling blue sea of the broadwater, or the splendid vista of countless highrise buildings set against a cloudless azure sky.

Australia's Gold Coast. Situated in south-east Queensland, it possessed a magic all its own, an elusive quality that brought tourists from around the world flocking in their thousands every year. Most came for the envied number of sunshine hours, winter and summer; others for the excellent surfing conditions. Whatever the reason, a casual holiday atmosphere abounded all year round, hinting at sun-soaked relaxation, with ample entertainment available. Accommodation ranged from budget-priced motels to exclusive luxurious apartments with every facility imaginable.

Names of various highrise buildings varied from the sublime to the exotic, and Rachel eased the Porsche to a halt outside a prestigious multi-storied block overlooking the ocean.

'Wow!' Millie murmured appreciatively as they rode the elevator to the twenty-fifth floor.

Emerging into the lushly-carpeted lobby Rachel checked the key-tab, then indicated the hall leading to the right.

Their apartment was large, its appointments luxurious, the pale spearmint-green and peach colour-scheme cool and refreshing.

'This is living,' Millie breathed ecstatically as she moved from one room to another. 'My God, look at that view!'

At the price they were paying per day, the view had to be magnificent, Rachel decided wryly, then immediately stifled her cynicism. They both earned good salaries, and could easily afford to indulge themselves.

'Which bed do you want?'

'I don't mind,' she shrugged easily. 'You choose.'

'Shall we unpack now, or leave it until later?'

Rachel wrinkled her nose expressively. 'If I say now, you'll never forgive me. What say we change into our bikinis, pull on a skirt and top, then walk through the main centre? We can have a drink, browse among the shops, then head for the beach.'

'Exactly what I hoped you'd say!'

Undoing her suitcase, she extracted what she needed, then pushed a towel, sunscreen lotion, and underwear into a carry-bag. Her bikini was little more then two miniscule scraps of yellow silk, and she slipped on a skirt, slid her arms into a short-sleeved muslin shirt and tied the lower edges together at her midriff. Slim wedge-heeled sandals on her feet, sunglasses resting on top of her hair, and she was ready.

The first few days were idyllic. The sun shone in a cloudless sky, its warmth fingering the sandy shores with gentle ease. Mid-October made for pleasant weather, with none of the hot humidity that abounded from December through to February. Now there was a breeze to temper the heat, making it all too easy to sunbathe comfortably for a few hours each morning. In the afternoon they browsed among the many shops or took in one of the theme parks, and because it was Millie's first visit, Rachel insisted they take a cruise round the canal estates. During the evening they took it in turns to choose some form of entertainment—a nightclub, a restaurant with a good floorshow, the cinema.

'How about having an evening at home?' Rachel suggested as they rode the elevator up to their apartment late Wednesday afternoon.

'Oh, but we can't,' Millie wailed swiftly. 'I've got tickets for a show.'

'At this rate, I'll be going back to work for a rest!'

The other girl's face fell slightly. 'Tomorrow night we'll just have dinner somewhere, then come back early. Promise—okay?'

'I'll take you up on that,' she assured as she selected a key and opened their apartment door. For some reason she felt edgy, and couldn't fathom the reason why. Trying to summon some enthusiasm she queried lightly, 'So, where is this show, and what time does it start?'

'Twin Towns Services Club at Tweed Heads at eight. Shall we eat before we leave, or have dinner there?'

'Here,' Rachel insisted quickly. 'You ring room service while I shower. Just a light snack for me—chicken and salad will do fine.'

Choosing what to wear created no problem, and she selected a slim-fitting white frock without hesitation. Its deep cowl neckline and thin shoestring straps showed her golden tan to advantage, and she added a slim gold belt to her waist. Make-up was kept to a minimum with lipgloss accentuating the fullness of her mouth, and skilful use of eyeshadow and mascara gave emphasis to her eyes. Slim-heeled gold strappy sandals added extra height, and she slid a number of gold bracelets over her wrist, then fastened an exquisite linked chain at her neck.

'You look terrific.'

She turned and gave a warm smile. 'You look pretty good yourself.'

'Average, to your stunning,' Millie responded without envy, and Rachel's eyes widened slightly.

Her mirrored image reflected a slim-waisted, softly-curved feminine form of average height.

Delicate fine-boned features were almost classical in appearance, her mouth generous, and wide-spaced blue eyes were the colour of sapphire, deepening or lightening with every mood-change. Dark blonde hair cascaded down her back to brush against her shoulders, sunstreaked in summer, its shining length owing nothing to artifice. It all added up to an attractive whole that she would have to be blind not to acknowledge, but—*stunning*?

'Shall we go?' she queried lightly, linking her arm through Millie's as they moved towards the door.

'I've yet to figure out why no man has snapped you up.'

'Maybe I don't want to be caught.'

'Several have tried,' Millie teased, and Rachel gave a wry smile as the elevator took them swiftly down to the car-park.

'I value my independence,' she managed evenly as she crossed to the bright yellow Porsche, and unlocking the passenger door she stepped round and slid in behind the wheel.

'Is it always like this?' Millie murmured almost an hour later as they stood in the Services Club reception area endeavouring to make their way through the crowd.

'A top-line artist must be performing tonight,' Rachel alluded wryly, narrowly avoiding a jostling elbow as the group beside her attempted to push through.

'There is. Didn't I tell you?'

They reached the curving stairs and slowly began to ascend. Rachel glimpsed the coloured poster advertisement as Millie announced with awed reverence.

'Laz Delany.'

The colour drained from her face, and for a moment she thought she was going to faint.

'Rachel? Is something wrong?'

Wrong. *Wrong?* She wanted to turn and run down the stairs, slip into her car and drive as far away from here as swiftly as possible.

'Rachel?'

Oh God. She wasn't conscious of Millie's hand on her arm, or the anxiety in her friend's pleasant features. 'I'm not feeling very well.' That was nothing less than the truth!

'Let's go and sit down,' Millie urged, clearly worried. 'I'll get you a drink.'

Get out of here—now. Make some excuse, but *go.* The words echoed and re-echoed as all her instinct screamed in agonised rejection.

'Is it a headache?'

She dragged her eyes from the poster, allowing herself to be led into a nearby bar, and minutes later a cool glass was pushed into her hand.

'I've got some aspirin in my bag.' Millie was already searching for them, extracting the slim strip of foil-enclosed tablets within seconds. 'Take a couple now, and by the time the show starts you'll probably feel okay.'

Mechanically Rachel swallowed one tablet and followed it with another, knowing they would have no effect whatever. Nothing would, except a powerful tranquilliser, and she no longer carried those mind-deadening pills.

In the beginning they had been a nesessity, and medically prescribed. It had taken six months before she'd gathered sufficient courage to dispense with them, a further six months to pick up the shattered pieces of her existence. One year of her life had been carefully locked away, never forgotten, but living with the memory had become easier—until now.

'Rachel?' Millie's voice intruded through the shadows of her mind. 'If you feel really lousy, we'll go back to the apartment.'

It was the perfect solution, and for a moment she almost agreed. Then determination stiffened her resolve. For nearly six years one man's ghost had ridden her shoulder. Maybe the time had come to lay it to rest.

'No.' Amazing how calm she sounded. 'I'm beginning to feel better already.'

'Are you sure?' The relief in Millie's voice was clearly audible, and Rachel summoned a faint smile in reassurance.

'Yes.'

At that precise moment an announcement was made through the club's intercom system, urging guests who held tickets for the show to make their way to the auditorium.

Her hand shook slightly as she lifted her glass and drained the remaining contents, then she stood to her feet before her courage could evaporate.

Rachel was glad of the innocuous chatter around her, for it precluded having to think, and ten minutes later a shaft of agony speared its way through her stomach as the lights dimmed, then the band came on, followed by the supporting act, heightening the tension to an unbearable degree.

Intermission became a suspended entity, and she had to physically school herself to remain seated as the music began.

It was an introduction to one of his most popular songs, the lead guitar strong and vibrant as a forerunner to Laz's entry on stage.

Then suddenly he was there—his mere presence an arresting electric force, projecting every superlative in male charisma.

Laz Delany. Composer, singer, *actor*.

Six years ago he had boarded the crest of the recording/performing wave. Now he was a superstar. Not only with the recording industry, but on the silver screen as well. A hot property that was instantly newsworthy wherever he went. If he so much as smiled, it made the supermarket tabloids.

Rachel closed her eyes against the sight of him, and a convulsive shiver shook her slim frame as he sang the first chord.

She knew the words by heart, their meaning indelibly imprinted in her brain. She should. He'd dedicated it to her as a birthday gift. Proclaiming every time he sang the song she would know it was his special way of touching, loving her.

Every woman felt the same, sensing its special significance as the melody wove an undeniable magic, elusive, tender, and sung in French it gained mysterious allure.

Now all the pain returned, tenfold, seeping into her bones until her whole body became one pulsing tormenting ache.

Staying here was madness, yet she didn't possess the power to rise to her feet and walk out.

'Isn't he gorgeous?' Millie whispered, totally enthralled by the embracing warmth of his voice, the physical aura he managed to exude without seeming effort.

Rachel wasn't capable of uttering so much as a word, and she sat still, almost afraid to move in case some unknown gesture would betray her inner turmoil.

The only lighting effects were several spots that arced over the audience in constantly-moving beams, and she was unaware of their exposing fingers until it was too late, then she was sitting in partial darkness again, wondering why she should suddenly feel isolated—almost *naked*. She was only one of many, her blonde hair similar to that of several other women in the audience. Besides, she knew the effortless ease with which Laz delivered each song required immense concentration. There was always the chance without it that he might develop a mental block and confuse the lyrics.

As well as his own songs, Laz sang a medley of popular ballads, two in French, another in Spanish.

Then it was over, until by tumultuous demand he returned on stage to render an encore. Afterwards the stage lights faded to darkness, and when the house lights came on Laz had gone.

'Wasn't he wonderful?'

Rachel dragged her eyes away from the empty stage and managed an inarticulate averral. She let the noise of chattering patrons envelop her, catching snatches of rapt feminine salutation and marvelled at her own disassociation.

God. She couldn't even think clearly, let alone *feel*. She was numb—emotionally, physically.

'Shall we go into the lounge for a drink? Maybe play the poker machines for a while?'

If she didn't get out of here soon, she'd become a mental wreck! 'I—would you mind if we went straight back to the apartment?' She lifted shaky fingers to her temple. 'My headache seems to have returned with a vengeance.'

Millie hid her disappointment well, and her

glance was full of concern. 'Do you want me to drive?'

They had almost reached the lobby, the queue of people slowing measurably as patrons mingled, undecided whether to try their luck on the machines downstairs, frequent the supper room, the bar, or simply call it a night and go home.

'Rachel.'

She stopped dead, unaware of the interested glances, and slowly let her eyes lift towards the owner of that Texan drawl.

'Hello, Mike.' She wasn't conscious of uttering a sound, but somehow the words had emerged in spite of her.

'I'll take you backstage.'

'No!' Her stomach began to heave as nervous tension manifested itself in a most unenviable manner. 'No,' she denied shakily, feeling all emotion drain from her body. So he had seen her. Or Mike, Brad, *Simi*. One of them had picked her out of the crowd.

'It's been a long time, Rachel,' he murmured persuasively.

She wanted to cry out that if she'd known Laz was performing, wild horses wouldn't have dragged her here. Instead, she said, 'I'm with a friend.'

Mike's gaze skimmed towards Millie, then returned, and he gave a faint shrug. 'Bring her along.'

'I can't.' Those two simply-spoken words were offered in helpless explanation, and as if to emphasise them, she shook her head in mute negation as she made to move past him.

'Laz will be disappointed.'

Brilliant pools of sapphire sparked briefly as she

swung back towards him. 'I'm sure he'll manage to live with it.'

'Where are you staying?'

'Oh no, Mike,' she decried softly, and the look she gave him was full of pitiless cynicism. 'I'm not that stupid.'

His smile was a mere facsimile. 'No messages?'

What did he expect after all this time? 'None.'

His eyes pierced hers, their regard almost hypnotic. 'Sure you won't change your mind?'

She shook her head, then mindful of Millie's stupefaction, she caught hold of her friend's arm and urged her towards the lobby.

'You *know* Laz Delany?' Millie queried in open amazement.

'Let's get out of here.' Rachel felt suddenly cold, and she began to shiver from delayed reaction.

'Rachel——'

'Later. I'll explain later.' Why did she feel as if a hundred demons were about to follow in pursuit?

They were downstairs and out into the cool night air before she was even aware of it, and she hurried towards her car with Millie almost running to keep the pace.

It wasn't until she'd fired the engine and was out of the town's main centre that she felt anywhere near at ease, and she sent the Porsche moving swiftly along the highway, reaching the outskirts of Surfer's Paradise in record time.

The stream of traffic was constant, and it was sheer nerves that caused her to check the rear-view mirror more frequently than necessary.

A hysterical laugh died in her throat. Laz would be caught up with the show's aftermath. When the exclusive favoured few invited backstage had departed, Laz would head to wherever they were staying and begin to unwind. Five years ago he'd travelled with an entourage of five, plus band. Success could only have increased that number measurably.

The highrise car-park lay ahead of them, and Rachel eased the sports car into the driveway, then paused to insert the garage key, watching as the door slid upwards before driving down to her allotted space.

They rode the elevator to their apartment, and once inside Rachel crossed to the kitchen cupboard, took out a glass and poured herself a stiff drink.

'I hardly dare ask,' Millie began stoically. 'But I'm going to, anyway. Just how well do you know Laz Delany?'

What was the use of prevaricating? It wasn't exactly common knowledge, but nor was it classified information. 'Very well.'

'How—*well*?'

Rachel moved into the lounge and prowled across to stare out the window. From this height the ocean looked dark and mysterious, its curving foreshore outlined by a steadily diminishing collection of lit apartment windows and street lights.

'I met him six years ago,' she revealed with detachment.

'And he persuaded you to have an affair?'

Rachel uttered a humourless laugh. 'Worse than that.'

'Good heavens,' Millie whispered, aghast. 'What could be worse?'

'Marriage.'

Stunned disbelief was visible in every line of Millie's body, and her face was nothing less than a caricature. 'Laz Delany—you—*married*?' She sank into the nearest chair, dumbfounded. 'What happened?'

'What happened that he married me?' She was being deliberately facetious, and Millie shook her head in silent remonstrance.

'Afterwards.'

'We separated.'

'That's it?'

'It's all you're going to get,' Rachel said quietly, and lifting the glass to her lips she drained the contents in one single swallow. 'Now, if you'll excuse me, I'm going to bed.'

She went through the motions of removing her make-up, cleaning her teeth, discarding clothes and donning a nightshirt with mechanical dedication before crossing to the bed.

The sheets were cool and crisp, and she lay her head on the pillow and closed her eyes, willing merciful oblivion. Except Laz's forceful image inhabited her brain, his undeniable magnetism demanding recognition.

A slow-burning fire began to invade her limbs and encompassed her whole being until she became caught up with a desire so intense, every pulse and pore in her body *ached* as it craved his possession.

Dear God—would she never be free of this torturous damning *torment*? It kept her awake nights, invading her subconscious to an extent where oft-occurring dreams assumed a nightmarish quality, and she would wake bathed in sweat, her body on fire and shaking, almost as if some devilish power was responsible for arousing physical desire to fever-pitch, then deliberately teased her into wakefulness to deal with an aftermath of desolation.

With a groan of despair Rachel rolled on to her stomach and pummelled the pillow.

Any attempt to separate the physical from prosaic reason was lost as words from Laz's love-song lilted insidiously in her mind, the music rippling gently in the background, the sound so hauntingly vivid she covered her ears against the sound of it.

If she'd been in her own room she could have switched on the light, turned on the bedside radio, then determinedly read until she fell asleep through sheer exhaustion.

Sharing a bedroom with Millie precluded any such escape, and gradually, with perfidious tenacity, the past five years began to melt away, and she closed her eyes in an effort to shut out the vivid clarity of enforced recollection.

CHAPTER TWO

IT had begun when Rachel auditioned for a television music special. The part was only small, but she was one of the few successful dancers selected for background choreography.

Rehearsals lasted several days before the actual taping, and it wasn't until dress rehearsal that the three guest singers appeared for a run-through with the rest of the cast.

Laz was magical on stage, his voice a deep mellifluous honey, and his handling of the slow ballads put him in a class all his own. In Sydney to tape the special, he was also appearing nightly at one of the inner city clubs.

In his early thirties, he was tall and muscularly lean, his features ruggedly attractive rather than classically handsome. Wide-spaced grey eyes held level clarity and a measure of self-assurance, although his mouth, even when immobile, possessed latent sensuality, promising a passionate warmth few women could successfully ignore. Dark brown hair bore casual grooming, and his clothes were worn with careless sophistication, generating the impression he was equally at ease wearing faded Levi's or a tuxedo.

In between his own numbers he stood to one side, quietly observant, looking every inch the dedicated professional.

It wasn't inevitable they should meet. In fact, Rachel hadn't expected him to even notice her. And when he did, proffering an invitation to share a coffee-break, she was torn between acceptance or polite refusal.

Even then, an intrinsic physical attraction was evident, and she found herself agreeing to visit a nearby café instead of the studio canteen when they both finished for the afternoon.

'Rachel,' Laz drawled slowly, his broad Atlantic accent giving it a slightly different intonation. 'Nice name, nice girl.'

'You don't know anything about me,' she said seriously, and he smiled.

'Enlighten me. How old you are, where you live, what you do in your spare time—and if you'll meet me after the show tonight.'

'Twenty,' she responded evenly, holding his steady gaze. 'Rose Bay, tennis and martial arts—and, no.'

His laughter was low and husky, and there was genuine humour in those dark grey depths. 'No?'

'We tape tomorrow. I need my share of beauty sleep.' She lifted her cup and held it in both hands, then sipped the hot black brew.

'I'll have a car pick you up at seven. It'll take you home straight afterwards. No strings.'

Her eyes were remarkably level. 'You're very persuasive.'

'Aren't I just?'

Slowly she replaced her cup, then she bent to gather up her bag. 'Thanks for the coffee.'

His gaze narrowed fractionally. 'I have the feeling I'm being let down.'

Rachel stood to her feet with fluid grace. 'A short meaningless relationship isn't my style,' she said simply, and even managed a faint smile. 'Somehow, I think that's exactly what you have in mind.'

'You know nothing about my mind,' he drawled quietly, and standing up he slid out his wallet, extracted a note and put it down on the table, then he caught hold of her elbow as she moved to slip past him.

'I have a bus to catch.' She wasn't angry, only incredibly sad.

'Then I'll see you to the bus stop.'

'But you don't know the city,' she protested, and he gave an indolent shrug.

'I know where I'm staying. I'll take a cab back.'

They walked in silence, and it lasted so long she didn't know how to break it without sounding inane. As they reached the bus shelter she turned slightly and met his faint brooding glance.

'Thanks for the coffee.'

'You already said that.'

Now she felt awkward. 'Good luck for the show tonight.'

His slanting smile contained a certain wryness. 'Enjoy your beauty sleep.'

The slow rumble of an engine heralded the arrival of her bus, and she moved to join the queue without so much as a backwards glance. Inside, she tendered her fare, then took the nearest vacant seat.

As the bus pulled out from the kerb she glanced across to where he stood, and saw his arm lift in a mocking salute.

It wasn't until after dinner that she leafed through the entertainment section of the daily newspaper, assuring herself it was just idle curiosity responsible for ascertaining where he was appearing. His face leapt from the page in startling black and white, the stark news-photo emphasising his smiling features. He was booked to appear until Saturday night. Four more days. After the taping session tomorrow, she'd probably never see him again.

Gruelling was the only fitting description as the choreographer put everyone through their paces next morning, and Rachel collapsed into the dressing-room afterwards feeling totally exhausted, yet exhilarated in the knowledge that all had gone well. She had caught a brief glimpse of Laz before the cameras rolled, and his lazy smile upset her composure, quickening her heartbeat to an alarming degree, so that she had to forcibly dispel his image to enable total concentration.

The following day she awoke to the insistent peal of the telephone, and she flew to answer it, only to discover Laz's manager asking if she could be ready in an hour.

'Why?' Rachel demanded baldly, trying valiantly to ignore the way her stomach was behaving over the fact that Laz had chosen to contact her, albeit indirectly.

'Laz wants to see something of Sydney, and would appreciate your company.'

She closed her eyes momentarily, then slowly opened them. 'How did you get my number?'

A deep chuckle came down the line. 'It only needed a few enquiries, honey.'

That did it! 'My name is Rachel,' she relayed with quiet dignity. 'And you woke me up.' Then she replaced the receiver.

Damn Laz Delany, damn his manager! Who did they think they were dealing with, for heaven's sake! A silly girl so besotted by star-status that she'd agree to anything?

An hour later there was a knock at the front door, and Laz stood framed behind the security-screen, a conspicuous sheaf of cellophane-encased roses in his hand.

'Are you always grumpy in the morning?'

Slowly she unlocked the door. 'I was annoyed,' she corrected steadily, feeling her heart trip its beat then begin to thud at an increasing rate as he directed her a slow lazy smile.

'Aren't you going to ask me in?'

'I'm not sure that I should.'

His grey eyes creased with humour as he held out the roses. 'I bought these for you.'

'A peace offering, or a persuasive ploy?'

'Both,' he alluded solemnly. 'I thought if I brought them in person and proffered my apologies, you just might be swayed into joining me for the day.'

Rachel looked at him in silence for a few seconds, then she ventured—'There has to be a thousand other girls who would jump at the chance.'

His gaze was startlingly direct. 'I'd rather have you.'

'That's supposed to be a reason why I should go out with you?'

His glance didn't waver. 'I'm sorry for getting Mike to do something I should have done myself.'

She held his gaze unflinchingly. 'Delegating must be a real chore.'

'It's a necessity if I want to give each performance my best, and get to sleep a minimum of six hours out of every twenty-four.'

'So you have a business manager to take care of financial matters, an agent to arrange your bookings, and a secretary to keep track of all the paperwork.'

The smile deepened slightly. 'You left out two,' Laz mocked gently, and her eyebrows rose a fraction.

'You mean there's more?'

'As long as you're listing them,' he slanted solemnly. 'You may as well add my personal manager and my public relations man.'

She wasn't capable of uttering a word, and after a few minutes he stepped through the doorway, placed the roses into the crook of her arm, closed the door, then pushed her gently down the hall.

'Do you live alone?'

'No.'

'Boyfriend? Girlfriend? Family?'

'My mother and sister,' she informed quietly.

They reached the kitchen, and he took the roses and moved towards the sink. 'Go and get a vase.'

By the time she'd retrieved it from a nearby cupboard he had the cellophane undone, and she watched as he stripped off the lower leaves, then filling the vase with water he carefully arranged the deep red flowering buds, one by one, before solemnly placing them down on to the bench.

'Now will you come out with me?'

Rachel looked at him for a few timeless minutes, seeing the easy strength apparent, the quiet forcefulness beneath his rugged exterior, then hesitated, unsure whether she should relent.

'If I say "please", will it make any difference?'

'I have to be back by five,' she capitulated at last, and glimpsed his sloping smile.

'Five, it is.'

For some reason she was unable to control her breathing, and to cover her confusion she glanced down at her jeans and jumper. 'I'll have to change.'

'You look fine to me.'

He was wearing casual clothes. Hip-hugging Levi's, and a cream vee-necked cable-knit jumper.

Shrugging, she crossed to the servery, retrieved a pad and penned a short note which she anchored with a colourful magnetic butterfly to the refrigerator. Then she collected a jacket, slid a few items into her bag, and preceded him to the front door.

A taxi stood waiting, and she turned with shocked surprise. 'You came in a *taxi*?'

Laz effected a careless shrug. 'How else would I get here?'

'You can't mean to hire his services for the rest of the day?' she queried, clearly scandalised.

'Why not? He knows all the scenic spots.'

She expelled her breath slowly. 'We'll use my car.'

'I came to take you out. Not the other way round,' he declared evenly, and she flung him an exasperated glance.

It was a day out of time, some special illusory gift each was almost afraid to accept, and Rachel never wanted it to end. Scorning the city, she drove first to Vaucluse, letting him view the majestic sweep of coves and inlets that formed Port Jackson. Next came the north shore, taking in French's Forest and all the eastern suburbs facing the Pacific Ocean. They had lunch at Palm Beach, picnic-fashion, with crusty bread rolls split and filled with sliced meat and salad, fresh fruit, and washed it all down with Perrier.

'It's good for the system,' Laz mocked lightly. 'Doesn't send you up or let you down.'

Rachel leaned back and watched him drain the glass bottle. 'You don't drink at all?'

'Not alcohol, except for the infrequent glass of quality champagne.'

'Or smoke?'

'Name any singer who cares about his voice that does,' he intoned drily, and she fell into silence.

'Hey,' Laz murmured gently. 'We're not all high-living, hell-raising freaks. I worked hard to get my feet on the first step of the ladder. Even harder, to climb steadily towards the top. I haven't quite reached it yet, but when I do, I'll fight to stay there, then quit while I'm ahead.'

'Quit?'

'Retire, is perhaps more apt.' His glance lanced hers, and she held it unwaveringly. 'I have a number of songs running through my head, lyrics. It's what I do best.' He effected a light shrug. 'When I think the time is right, I'll seclude myself somewhere and compose.'

'It sounds idyllic.'

'I plan to make it just that.'

She swallowed, feeling suddenly bereft that she would share no part of it, and summoning immense courage she queried with seeming lightness—'Laz—it's an unusual name. Is it your own?'

'My parents are French-Canadian, and I was christened Lazare Michel Delany. Whereas Lazare Delany becomes something of a mouthful, *Laz* Delany rolls off the tongue with fluid ease.'

'Where do you go after Sydney?' Rachel asked idly.

'The Gold Coast for three nights, then back to the States.'

She felt restless, unable to shake off the beginnings of an intrinsic, almost elemental fascination this man held for her. If she didn't put some distance between them, she'd be lost. Slowly she rose to her feet, her expression polite. 'Shall we go.'

His eyes were brilliant, and far too discerning for comfort. 'What's the hurry?'

'There's an awful lot to see.'

'The scenic trip was just an excuse to have you spend the day with me.'

The breath caught in her throat, and she swallowed convulsively. 'I already guessed that. What I haven't worked out is why you're so bent on wasting your time.'

'I enjoy your company.'

'You don't know me.'

His voice was even, his gaze steady. 'I'd like to.'

'So I can become "Rachel in Sydney" in your diary? Or perhaps you don't bother trying to remember after a week.'

Without a word he stood to his feet, then bent to gather up the remains of their lunch. 'Let's go.'

Where? Was this the end of it all?

'You were going to show me the sights of Sydney,' Laz prompted imperturbably, and in a daze she turned towards the car, glad of the long curtain of hair falling forward as she moved, masking her expression.

When she slid the car to a halt outside the entrance to his hotel a few hours later he made no immediate effort to get out.

'If I offer you a ticket for the show tonight, will you throw it back in my face?'

Her lashes lowered in defence against the subtle persuasion in his voice. 'It's very kind of you, but—no, thank you,' she refused carefully, and missed the slight wry twist of his lips.

'Tomorrow night?'

She looked at him then, her eyes wide and clear. 'Why?'

'Because it would give me pleasure to know

you're out there in the audience.'

Dare she? 'My mother and my sister enjoy your music.' There was safety in numbers.

'I'll see that three tickets are left at the desk.' Depressing the door-clasp he eased his lengthy frame out from the seat. '*Au revoir*, Rachel.'

Their seats were exceptionally good—front row, centre, and Rachel wondered if Laz insisted a certain number were left empty for 'girlfriends'. Somehow the thought made her uncomfortable, almost as if her mere presence signified an acceptance of some sort.

It coloured her thinking, and spoilt what otherwise would have been a pleasurable evening.

Just before the final number a man materialised from back-stage. 'Mike Adamson, Laz's personal manager.' He spoke quietly, but his voice managed to penetrate sufficiently to be heard above the music. 'Laz would like you to join him after the show. There's a limousine outside the rear exit, if you'll follow me?'

Rachel wanted to refuse, but Rebecca's enthusiastic response, coupled with her mother's, made it impossible.

Engine purring in readiness, the large car was nothing less than opulent, its expensive leather seats the epitome of luxurious comfort.

Five minutes later Laz slipped in beside the driver, and the vehicle surged forward, negotiating the inner city streets with ease before pulling to a halt outside the hotel's rear entrance.

Another vehicle, equally long and black, parked behind them, and there was the sound of doors slamming, voices, then a tap on the window.

'All clear, Mr Delany.'

'Sorry,' Laz apologised. 'A necessity, I'm afraid.

You three go first. Mike will escort you. I'll follow in a few minutes.'

Even as they alighted, fans began to converge, and Mike encouraged quickly.

'Move, ladies. A few more seconds, and you won't have the opportunity.'

'What about Laz?' Rachel murmured, faintly bemused, as they were hurried indoors, and caught Mike's wry expression.

'The two chauffeurs are hired bodyguards, employed to hover discreetly while Laz signs a few autographs. After five minutes, Brad and Pete will converge, and Laz will regretfully attempt to move inside.' He crossed to the elevator and punched a button, his glance moving to the indicator light. 'The bodyguards will ensure the fans stay quiet while Brad, Zeke and Pete flank Laz into the lobby, then remain downstairs to ensure no one follows him.'

'It's just like in the movies,' Rebecca breathed with awe, and Mrs Devison cast her elder daughter a probing glance.

Rachel wanted to tell Mike to stop the elevator, say they'd changed their minds. But to do so would seem not only churlish, but childish. Besides, it was too late. If they were going to refuse, they should have done so at the start.

The suite of rooms into which Mike directed them was breathtaking, and waiting, her oriental features carefully composed, was a woman whose age could have ranged anywhere between twenty-five and forty.

'This is Simi,' Mike introduced carelessly. 'Laz's secretary.'

Set to one side was an elaborately-set table with champagne in ice-buckets, Perrier, bottled wine and spirits, and a number of salads, a collation of cold meats and chicken, fresh fruit and a cheese board. There was also percolated coffee.

A feast fit for a king and his minions, Rachel decided wryly, wondering what on earth possessed her to come.

Simi went into action as a gracious hostess, plying them with drink, urging them to try something from the display of food. She was good, very good; welcoming, but scarcely friendly.

Laz's entry into the suite came some ten or fifteen minutes later, and he accepted the glass Simi handed him before crossing to converse with his three guests.

He was devastating, yet it didn't seem contrived. In fact, he seemed to work very hard to dispel the 'star' image. Yet it was there, just the same. Indefinable magic, charisma, machismo—magnetic sexuality. He had it all, plus an undeniable talent. Packaged and promoted into a money-spinning commodity that filled theatres and clubs, sold tickets, and brought personal fame and fortune.

They stayed for an hour. Not once during that time did he attempt to touch her, although his eyes were warm whenever they rested on her—warm and infinitely intimate. Almost as if he was trying to indicate they didn't *need* words. That they could be alone, mentally attuned to each other, in a room full of people.

It was crazy. Not only crazy, but dangerous. To lose her heart to someone of Laz Delany's calibre would be akin to riding a truck laden with nitroglycerine. She might make the journey in one piece—then again, she might not! It wasn't a gamble she wanted to take.

Mike rode the elevator down to the ground floor, then he escorted them into the waiting limousine. 'Tell the driver where you want to go.'

Back to the car-park to collect their car, and no one said so much as a word during that short chauffeur-driven journey.

Afterwards the questions came and Rachel fielded them as best she could all the way home.

Laz 'phoned the next morning, his voice a low husky drawl that succeeded in stirring every nerve-end into tingling vibrant life.

'There's a party after the final show. I'd like you to be there.'

Direct and to the point, with no wasted verbiage. Rachel's grip on the receiver tightened. 'I don't think it would be a good idea,' she managed after a measurable silence. She could visualise it even now. Champagne, beautiful plastic people intent on outdoing each other. She'd be like a fish out of water.

'I'm needed at the television studio to film a commercial, and tomorrow is taken up with business.' He sounded vaguely impatient, even irritated. 'Dammit, I don't have the time——' he broke off, then murmured quietly—'I'll have a car pick you up from home at ten. Come—please.'

Wisdom had nothing to do with her decision to go, and more than once she crossed to the 'phone determined to cancel out. Except she never picked up the receiver to make the call.

The club was filled to capacity as she took her seat just as the lights faded after interval, and the numbers Laz chose to sing were a collection of favourites, with one exception. It came last in the final bracket, and was unashamedly a love song. What's more, his eyes never left her face—not even once. The audience stirred as it sensed the rendition had a special significance, and Rachel felt she was the cynosure of all eyes.

As the band carried the last few chords, Mike materialised at her side, and she stood to her feet, following him back-stage with the movements of an automaton, feeling as conspicuous as a solitary glow-worm in an unlit cave.

Laz had already changed by the time she entered his dressing-room, and she registered dully that he must be an expert in discarding and pulling on clothes.

'Five minutes,' Mike declared, and Laz nodded, his eyes narrowing slightly as she refused to meet his gaze.

'Rachel.' His voice was quiet, yet held a hint of steel, and when she didn't answer, he crossed the small room in three easy strides.

A hand reached for her chin, taking it between thumb and forefinger, lifting it so she had little choice but to look at him. She tried to mask her expression without success, and he muttered a husky oath, then caught hold of her shoulders.

'For Christ's sake, don't look like that,' Laz groaned softly, then his head lowered and his mouth settled on hers with gentle possessiveness.

Rachel felt her body tremble as a slow warmth coursed through her veins, bringing alive a multitude of sensations she was loath to explore. There was only *now*, and the singing, pulsing awareness that swept her up and tossed her high on to a plateau where sheer sensation ruled, until Laz reluctantly broke the kiss.

'We have to leave.' His eyes were dark with a deep slumbrous warmth, and his mouth curved into a slight smile as he lifted a hand to tuck one stray tendril of hair back behind her ear.

She could only look at him wordlessly, unable to assimilate a single rational thought, and she clung to his shoulders, the feel of warm muscled sinew beneath her fingers reassuring. She sensed rather than heard his swift intake of breath, then his mouth was on hers, hard and passionately demanding, his arms moulding her close, until she felt as if she was being *absorbed*, body and soul.

Then she was free, and the loud thudding in her ears turned out to be someone knocking on the door.

'Come with me when we move on to the Coast,' Laz insisted emotively, and Rachel felt as if she'd suddenly skated on to thin ice, knowing precisely what an acceptance would entail.

Three days. And after that—what? Goodbye, it was great? 'No.'

'For Chrissakes, Laz. Move it.'

'We have to leave—otherwise all hell will break loose,' Laz declared grimly, taking her arm and all but pulling her in his wake.

The black limousine was waiting, engine running, outside the rear entrance, and the chauffeur sent the vehicle surging forward the instant they were seated.

At the hotel, they went through the same routine, with Mike escorting Rachel inside, leaving Laz to deal with a barrage of waiting fans.

Simi greeted her with a slight degree of warmth, insisting on taking her coat as Mike stationed himself at the door.

Within minutes the guests began to arrive, and Rachel stayed close to Simi, feeling helpless and way out of her depth.

Laz's entrance caused a furore, and she watched as he paused to talk with one guest after another, circulating with sophisticated ease until he'd spoken to everyone in the room. Then he crossed to her side, and didn't leave it for the few hours she was there.

Speculation was rife, and she'd have had to be blind not to be aware of the circumspect glances she received as she sipped excellent champagne diluted with fresh orange juice and nibbled a few morsels from the abundance of food available.

The party looked as if it would go on until dawn, and at two Rachel indicated her intention to leave.

Laz gave her a swift glance, and seemed on the verge of refusing to let her go. 'I can't persuade you to stay?'

All too easily, Rachel thought sadly, shaking her head. She couldn't speak, she didn't trust her voice to remain steady.

'Mike will alert the chauffeur, and have you driven home.'

Simi fetched her coat at Laz's request, and raised her eyebrows slightly as Laz drew Rachel out of the suite towards the lift.

This is it, Rachel decided as she stood silently waiting for that electronic carriage. The magic bubble is about to burst.

What did she say? A simple 'thanks' seemed horribly banal.

Knowing him had been like nothing she'd experienced before, and she felt incredibly sad. Maybe if he was Lazare Delany this elusive awareness they shared might lead somewhere. But as *Laz* Delany, any romance didn't stand a chance of survival.

'Good luck with the rest of your tour.' The words sounded stilted and polite, and he made no attempt to stop her as she stepped into the waiting lift. Her eyes met his, then the doors slid closed.

Four days later Rachel returned home after a particularly exhausting practice-session to find an expensive piece of luggage in the hall, and Rebecca's breathless voice announcing Laz was to stay a few days before he flew out to the States.

Shock, helpless anger, and sheer nervous tension fought for supremacy as she crossed the room and sank down into the nearest chair. It was a cruel joke—it had to be. 'Where is he?'

'Here,' Laz drawled softly from the open doorway.

Dear God, she was hallucinating. If she hadn't been sitting down, she would have fallen. Closing her eyes against the sight of him did no good at all, for when she opened them he was close, bending over her, then catching hold of her hands he drew her out of the chair and into his arms.

For an age he simply held her, then his lips began a slow evocative exploration, travelling from her temple down the edge of her jaw to her mouth, outlining its trembling curve, brushing gently against its flowering warmth before trailing slowly up to caress each eyelid in turn.

When he kissed her she began to cry, silently, the slow warm tears trickling down to her chin, and he paused, tasting, savouring each rivulet until she begged him to stop.

Later the questions inside her head clamoured for an answer, demanding reason, except every time she found the courage to ask, the words refused to emerge.

Three days. They didn't leave the house once. Laughing, loving, growing together, the fascination Rachel felt rapidly developed into something deeper, nurtured by the strength of Laz's passionate restraint. It was almost as if he was trying to buy time, and his purpose was obscure until a few hours before he was due to fly out to Los Angeles.

'The very nature of my lifestyle precludes anything approaching a normal courtship,' he began seriously, and she was unable to utter so much as a word as he continued—'It may not be the right time or the right place——' he paused imperceptibly, his eyes clear and totally without cynicism. 'I want you in my life. To restore a sense of sanity in the madness that surrounds me. I could use any number of trite phrases in an attempt to convince you. Words, lyrics—I know them off by heart. If *loving* means you occupy my thoughts day and night, almost to the exclusion of everything else—the need I feel inside me—then, I love you.'

Rachel slowly found her voice, and to her surprise it sounded remarkably calm. 'I won't be your—travelling companion.'

'Idiot,' he chided with husky laughter. 'I'm asking you to marry me!'

Marriage? 'I've only known you for two weeks,' she choked shakily.

'I'll be back in a month,' Laz declared gently, reaching out to cup her face. 'We'll get married here, honeymoon in Acapulco, then we go on tour.'

'You're going too fast.' She felt as if she'd been picked up by a high-crested wave and was unsure she could land on her feet in safe water.

'Perhaps,' he allowed broodingly. 'For you. I've lived for years making split-second decisions, trusting my instincts. If I were to choose the right time to marry, it would be five—six years from now. Then I would be home several months out of twelve in every year. I would ask you to have my child, knowing I could give you both a sense of permanence. *Now* I have an obligation to my public—one I have no right to sever. Can you accept that?'

'Share you with a thousand women?' A slightly hollow laugh bubbled up from her throat. 'A million? It's asking an awful lot.'

'You will have my heart. Is it enough?'

Was it? Dare she take the risk? Weather what the next six years might bring, secure in the knowledge that at the end of that time the merry-go-round of tours, shows, wildly-ecstatic crowds of fans would be behind them.

Yet the loneliness of waiting, maybe losing him, was more than she could bear.

'I'm frightened,' she whispered, and he gathered her close, his arms enveloping her like a protective shield.

'Don't be.' His lips brushed her temple, then slid down the curve of her cheek, slipping lower until he found her mouth. 'I'll be there with you—every inch of the way.'

They were married a month later, a small church ceremony with only close relatives attending, and afterwards they flew to Mexico.

Mrs Laz Delany. Rachel Delany. It had a nice sound. They showered and changed in the hotel after the long flight, then ordered room service, eating the elaborate meal slowly, washing the food down with *Dom Perignon*. Then Laz stood to his feet, his eyes warm and slumbrous as she unhesitatingly took his hand, and their loving was everything Rachel had dreamed, and more. And long afterwards Laz made love to her again, slowly and with such infinite gentleness she cried, whispering his name over and over again as he transported her higher than she'd ever thought it possible to climb.

One week. One ecstatic, exquisite week of loving, discovering. Then came reality.

Laz's home was an apartment high above the city. Except he didn't live there for more than one week in every ten or twelve. Hotel rooms, luxurious suites, in one city or another, clothes forever being packed, unpacked. Room service became an oft-repeated phrase, and meals eaten out were a rarity that were more often than not marred by countless interruptions from starry-eyed fans.

Three months after their marriage, on the night of her twenty-first birthday, he started the show with a song dedicated to 'my wife, Rachel'. A slow ballad, lilting and poignant, sung in French, became a public declaration that brought tears to her eyes—and more than half the audience, from the wild ecstatic response it received.

'It's how I feel,' Laz vowed softly in the early hours of the morning, holding her close. 'I look at you, and you're everything I ever wanted. More than I deserve.' His kiss succeeded in melting her into a thousand pieces. 'You're the only sane thing in my life. Sometimes I become afraid the trappings, the fantasy, will eventually get to you and you'll want to leave. It can be scarey, performing before hundreds—sometimes *thousands*. Sharing a magic you're scarcely aware of, giving pleasure and getting it in return via audience gratification. It's a two-way thing that can be difficult to control. Knowing nine out of every ten women out there think you're singing just for them. On stage you're not an ordinary mortal, you're a figment of their imagination, fashioned in their mind. There is no such thing as identity. You become a 'star'. Packaged and presented as a commercial commodity. Publicity spins a web of intrigue, and sheer talent does the rest. The danger lies in believing any of it.'

Rachael vowed softly— 'I love you. I always will.'

She had honestly believed their love was special, and in her innocence she imagined it to be inviolate.

Loving Laz was easy. Living with what he represented became gradually impossible. Perhaps if she hadn't loved him so much she could have accepted the constant interruptions, the invasion of the media, the almost fanatical hysteria of the audience. The gossip linking his name with a number of women became increasingly difficult to ignore, as did the steady undermining of her self-confidence. Laz's world wasn't her world, and Simi rarely let her forget it.

It took a year for the disillusion to become complete, another month to reach and act upon the decision to leave.

When one of the major television studios offered Laz a contract for a series pilot, Rachel added her reassurance to that of Mike, Zeke and Brad, then when it was signed she carefully packed her bags, using the sudden onset of a gastro-virus as an excuse not to attend that night's show.

Within an hour of Laz leaving the apartment, she was boarding an international flight bound for Sydney. The note she'd penned him was pitifully brief, wishing him every success, and signing it simply 'love, Rachel'.

She didn't warn her mother or Rebecca, for it was essential their shocked surprise should sound genuine when Laz contacted them, as she knew he would. It would buy her a few days in which to see them, then make immediate plans to depart for another Australian State.

That was exactly what she did, steadily refusing to reveal the various reasons for their separation. And so her mother and Rebecca didn't have to lie on her behalf, she never gave them an address, only a 'phone number which she swore them to secrecy over, and arranged for all her mail to be collected at a central post office. Trans-Atlantic calls from Laz became less frequent after her mother managed to convince him she knew little of her daughter's whereabouts. And the letters forwarded on ceased after a few months, except for a single red silk rose accompanied by a card that appeared every Christmas and for her birthday each year. Nothing elaborate, just a printed verse, and signed 'love, Laz'.

Slowly she'd managed to rebuild her life, forsaking stage and television work for that of instructor at exercise classes and sports clinics.

Over the years Laz's face leapt from pages of countless magazines, then he began to grace the covers as his acting credibility ascended to unbelievable heights in a hit series. Wherever he went, whoever he was with, it made instant news. He appeared to have it all. Fame, fortune, and any number of women he wanted. Yet in every interview he'd granted, any mention of his private life was vetoed, and if a reporter dared relate a query regarding his marital status the answer was inevitably a bleak—'my wife and I are estranged'.

Every so often Rachel expected legal notification

of impending divorce proceedings, but no such letter ever reached her, and she began to conclude it suited him to use her elusive existence as a shield with his so-called companions.

Never in her wildest imagination did she envisage seeing him again.

CHAPTER THREE

'RACHEL! Wake up. It's past nine already.'

Rachel raised her head from the pillow, took in the bright morning sunlight streaming through the window, Millie's anxious, slightly puzzled features, and stifled an inaudible groan.

'I let you sleep, because I thought seeing your— Laz, again, might upset you.'

As a one-liner intended to bring forth some revealing comment, it failed dismally, and after a few minutes Millie resorted to the obvious.

'It's beautiful outside. Let's go down to the beach and sunbathe for a few hours. This afternoon we can take one of the tours, or stroll round the shops.'

How did she say that she wanted to stay where she was. Perhaps not in bed, but in the apartment and out of sight. Except to do so would be ridiculous. If Laz wanted to find her it wouldn't be difficult. She had registered under her maiden name, and Mike, under Laz's instructions, could be guaranteed to apply unstinting diligence to the task.

This was his first Australian tour in five years. Five years and two months to be precise—give or take a day or two. The knowledge confounded her, proving it was possible for one's brain to calculate without conscious application.

'I'll have a quick shower,' Rachel indicated, sliding out from the covers. Hell, she felt tired, enervated beyond belief. Maybe lying on the beach beneath the sun's warmth would do her good. She could doze, then refresh herself with a swim in the cool pulsing surf.

'I've already fixed your orange juice,' Millie declared. 'I'll make some fresh coffee and toast.'

They left the apartment building half an hour later, and crossed the road to the beach choosing a stretch of sand well away from other sunbathers to spread their towels.

Rachel lay on her back, every inch of exposed skin protected with sunscreen. Thirty minutes, then she would turn on to her stomach and doze.

'Shall I switch on the radio? Or do you want to talk?'

'Let's have some music,' she responded quietly, and heard Millie's audible sigh.

The sun's warmth had a soothing effect, lulling her into a state of relaxation, and it was more than an hour before she rose slowly to her feet and walked down to the sea, watching the waves as they crashed down and spilled towards the shore in a spuming mass of foam and spray.

Choosing her moment, she dived neatly into the water, then surfaced and began to coast in to shore on an incoming wave. Standing upright, she made her way on to the wet sand, pausing to wring excess moisture from her hair before walking back to gether up her towel.

'That was good. Do you want to go in?'

Millie shook her head in silent negation. 'I'm no swimmer, and besides, it looks a bit rough out there for me.'

'Shall we go back?' Rachel queried. 'We can shower and change, then have lunch in town.'

A strange prickling sensation feathered its way down her spine as they entered the foyer, and she suppressed a shiver as the elevator transported them to their designated floor.

Inside the apartment she closed the door and tried to dispel the faint air of foreboding that seemed to settle on her slim shoulders.

'I'll take the shower first,' she indicated, lifting a hand to her wet hair. 'I'll have to wash this. While I'm blowdrying it, you can have your shower, then we'll both be ready about the same time.'

Ten minutes later she turned off the jet of water, towelled herself dry, then slipped into a silk robe before giving attention to her hair.

Emerging from the bedroom she picked up the blowdrier, then called to Millie that the bathroom was free.

There was no sound from the lounge, and she moved out from the room, only to come to an abrupt halt at the sight of the slightly dazed expression on her friend's features. 'Millie?'

'Hello, Rachel.'

Oh God—*Laz*.

She seemed to freeze, locked into immobility by the sound of his voice, and her eyes flew straight to his, their sapphire depths widening and deepening with the shock of seeing him standing less than a few feet away.

Five years had wrought a few subtle changes. The grooves that slashed his cheeks seemed more deeply etched, and the tiny lines fanning out from the corners of his eyes were more noticeable. The breadth of his shoulders seemed even broader, and he looked incredibly fit, and the short-sleeved navy cotton shirt accentuating his tan, the grey of his eyes.

'Don't I even rate *hello*?'

It seemed superfluous to ask what he was doing

here. Ridiculous to query *why*. She hadn't been able to cope with seeing him last night on stage. Now in the confines of the apartment lounge it was a thousand times worse than she'd ever imagined.

'Hello, Laz.' There, she'd said it, her voice quietly calm and betraying none of the inner turmoil that wracked her nerves and tore her composure to shreds.

God. She had to steel herself from forgetting all the reasons why she'd left him. The five years melted away, dispensed in an instant as if they were of no consequence whatever.

'I'll go and shower.' Millie's words intruded, hesitant and faintly embarrassed. 'I'm sure you have a lot to talk about.' Then she fled, and Rachel felt her stomach muscles clench into a painful knot.

The moment she'd dreaded, lain bathed in sweat over on countless sleepless nights, had finally arrived.

'I guess I have Mike to thank—or damn, for this,' she managed evenly, fixing her gaze on the skyline beyond the nearby window. She could no longer look at him, his presence was too potent a force for her to adequately deal with.

'Why didn't you answer my letters?'

Could she pretend they never reached her? Or worse, admit she'd never opened them?

'What good would it have done?' She effected a slight shrug, and fought to control the faint trembling of her mouth. 'There was no room for me in your life.'

His eyes pinned her, lancing through the defensive barrier she'd erected as a protective shield, until it seemed as if her soul lay bare beneath the intensity of his gaze.

Rachel swallowed the convulsive lump that suddenly rose in her throat. 'We should never have married. At least, not then,' she corrected slowly, not daring to look at him. 'Maybe not ever.'

'Yet we did.' Laz moved slightly, thrusting hands into his trouser pockets, his expression becoming grim and forbidding. 'I tried damned hard to separate the fantasy.'

She lifted a hand and smoothed back the damp tendrils of hair that had fallen forward. 'The trouble was your fans never let you.' Her voice sounded strange, almost alien, and she listened to the words dispassionately, like a disembodied spectator. 'They were always *there*. Even the privacy of our own suite was not immune from various calls or visits from Mike, Zeke, Brad, Pete or Simi. I had to stand in line for a portion of your time; unsure, except in bed, whether I had a right to deserve any of it,' she said sadly. It took immense courage to meet and hold his gaze, but she succeeded. 'So—why are you here, now? What do you want?' She had to say it, even though it almost killed her. 'A divorce?'

'No.'

Her eyes became cloudy with pain as she recognised the inflexibility of his decision.

'You came to the show last night.'

'I didn't know you were appearing!'

'Er—excuse me,' Millie's startled voice intruded, and they both swung towards her. 'I'll go and browse among the shops for a few hours.' She looked from one to the other of them, then bolted for the door. 'G'bye.'

Rachel started to call out to stop her, then gave a helpless shrug as she thought better of it.

'Millie bought the tickets,' she revealed, seconds

after the door closed, her gaze remarkably clear. 'I found out you were the main attraction only minutes before the show was due to start.'

Grey eyes pierced hers, their depths unfathomable. 'Yet you stayed.'

'Only because I wanted to exorcise a ghost!'

'Were you successful?'

No, damn you! she cried silently, closing her eyes against the sight of him. When she opened them he was close, much too close for her peace of mind, and she took a backwards step in an attempt to put some distance between them.

'Five years, Rachel,' Laz drawled. 'You can't have been lonely.'

She shook her head in silent negation, her voice becoming heavy with weary cynicism. 'Oh, I dated, Laz. Men who vowed all they wanted was friendship, then became unjustifiably indignant when the evening didn't end the way they expected.' Her expression assumed wry hauteur. 'What do you want? A résumé of every man I've gone out with? How he kissed, how I felt when he tried to make out?'

For a moment his eyes filled with incredible anger, then it was successfully masked. 'Does it help to twist the knife?'

'Did you ever think how much *I* hurt?' she cried in anguish, so enraged she could have hit him.

'Yes,' he admitted heavily. 'Every day.'

'If I believed a tenth of your publicity,' Rachel declared bitterly. 'You wined, dined and bedded a bevy of beautiful young things.'

'They were none of them *you*.'

'That's meant to be *reassurance*?'

The breath seemed to force itself from his body in an impatient, pent-up hiss, as he controlled himself with apparent difficulty.

'What do you want?' Laz bit harshly. 'An avowal of celibacy?'

She was breathing hard, her heartbeat thudding loudly in her chest. 'I don't want anything from you, except to get out of my life!'

His silence had an unnerving effect, and his face became an expressionless mask. 'No way, Rachel.'

Her breath seemed to choke in her throat. 'What do you mean—*no way*?' The anger inside welled up with explosive force, making itself evident in the brilliance of her eyes, the barely-leashed tension emanating from her body. 'You can't expect to——'

'Take up where we left off,' he intervened silkily.

Her eyes widened, then became stricken with pain, and she began to shake with the effects of suppressed emotion—so much so, she crossed her arms across her body in an attempt to exert a measure of control. 'Never in a million years.'

'Was it so bad?'

Remembering how *good* it had been was almost her undoing. Except she'd had five years to reflect. Endless dark hours when she'd tossed and turned unable to sleep as she re-examined every factor for and against her decision.

'Shall I refresh your memory?' His voice was velvet-smooth and dangerously soft.

'No!' She moved back involuntarily as if physically threatened, afraid that any contact would dissolve the tenuous hold she retained on her emotions.

'So adamant,' Laz drawled, his eyelids lowering slightly as he assessed her reaction, and she watched with a kind of stupefied fascination as his hands closed over her shoulders.

His head lowered, then his mouth was on hers,

hard and possessively demanding as he sought to invade the soft inner sweetness, exerting sufficient pressure until unbidden, her jaw relaxed and allowed him entry.

Hands slid from her shoulders, down her back to enfold her close against the hard male contours of his body, then his mouth softened, gentling as he tasted the swollen fullness of her lips, tracing their provocative outline before slipping to caress the soft hollows at the base of her throat.

Not content, he followed the pulsing cord at the edge of her neck, then trailed to an earlobe, letting his tongue trace each ridge and hollow before slipping along the edge of her jaw to reclaim her lips.

Somehow her hands slid up to his shoulders, then slipped further to clasp together at his nape. Her fingers shook slightly as they came into contact with the springy softness of his hair, and she felt a shudder shake through his frame.

Somehow her silken robe no longer covered her, and she felt a slow tinge of colour flood her cheeks beneath the hunger of his gaze.

'You're even more beautiful than I remember,' Laz husked gently, trailing evocative fingers across the burgeoning peaks of her breasts, then slipped lower to trace the outline of her hips, the flatness of her stomach, before moving up to cup her face.

Oh God, what was she thinking of, letting him kiss her, touch her. It could only re-open old scars, intensify the heartache she'd weathered and somehow survived.

'*No*!' she cried desperately as he swung her into his arms and began walking towards the bedroom. 'Laz—don't. Please.' Dear heaven, she was begging, pleading with him, warm tears filling her eyes, making them resemble large tragic pools of shimmering sapphire. She began to shake as he came to a halt beside the bed, the breath emerging from her body in shuddering gasps. 'You can't do this to me. You *can't*.'

He let her slide down to her feet, his hands moving down her back, enfolding her close against him, and she buried her head against the curve of his throat.

How long she stayed there she had no idea, for she was only aware of the strength of his arms as he held her, the featherlight touch of his lips at her temples, on her eyelids, then finally her mouth.

'Don't ask me to leave.'

'You can't stay,' Rachel said slowly, raising her head to glimpse his dark questioning gaze.

'I'm your husband—remember?'

'That has nothing to do with it,' she murmured sadly, and his mouth moved to form a wry smile.

'No?'

She felt strangely vulnerable, at odds with the dictates of her traitorous body, and frighteningly aware just how easy it would be to let him love her. She even wanted it. Lord, so much, the longing for his possession was driving her insane.

'You can't just walk back into my life again.' She had to move away from him, put on some clothes.

'You walked out of mine.' There was an indefinable quality in his voice, almost a rawness, but he didn't attempt to restrain her as she slipped out of his grasp and crossed to the wardrobe.

Her hands shook as she extracted bra and briefs and slipped them on, then she stepped into white cotton trousers and selected a watermelon-pink top from its hanger.

Rachel was aware of him watching her every move, and she forced herself to breathe steadily to deploy the agitation she felt must be evident.

Her hair was damp, and she plugged in the blowdrier, stroking the brush through its tawny length until it flowed down on to her shoulders in a mass of golden curls.

'Don't—look at me like that,' she murmured unevenly, aware of the deep thudding beat of her heart.

'How would you have me look at you?' Laz slanted emotively.

'Let's go into the lounge.' She studiously avoided looking at him, choosing instead to fix her attention on a point beyond his left shoulder. 'We can talk there.'

Surprisingly he made no demur, and she felt awkward, intimidated by the sheer animal magnetism he exuded.

When they reached the lounge it took considerable effort to school her voice into polite civility. 'Why don't you sit down?' She indicated a nearby chair, then clasped her hands, twisting her fingers together. 'Can I get you something to drink? Coffee?'

One eyebrow rose slightly as he shot her a dark probing glance. 'I'm not some casual visitor,' he drawled, and a tinge of colour crept over her cheeks.

'I can't see a purpose to any of this,' Rachel declared wretchedly.

Laz moved across to stand by the large window, his attention seemingly caught by the wide expanse of ocean foreshore curving south until it became lost on the horizon.

'Five years ago I wanted to wring your lovely

neck,' he revealed slowly, not turning to look at her. 'If I'd been successful in finding you then, I'd have dragged you back by the hair of your head.' His shoulders lifted slightly as he released a heavy sigh. 'Now, I'm asking.'

'I can't,' she whispered, her eyes stricken, and he turned to face her, his expression bleak, the grey of his eyes almost black with intensity.

'I'm not renewing my contract for the television series. Apart from a few live performances, I'll be out of the public eye for several months a year.'

Rachel shook her head slowly. 'You've reached the zenith of your career. Mike, or Brad, or Zeke won't let you stop.' Her gaze was remarkably steady. 'It's like a merry-go-round, Laz. Once you're on, you can't get off.' She lifted a hand and smoothed back a stray tendril of hair, then let her hand fall back to her side. It was a nervous gesture, and it irked unbearably that he was aware of the effect he caused. 'Your fans will never let you go.'

He raked impatient fingers through his hair, regarding her with a degree of angry frustration. 'The television series was fun to do—while it lasted. But there's no way I want to be around in twenty years' time, trying vainly to recapture the time when I was on top. I enjoy singing, but writing music takes priority.' His expression hardened into an impenetrable mask. 'I've given my fans ten years of my life, at great personal sacrifice. They'll have to accept my decision.'

'Nothing will be different,' she evinced shakily. 'It might take months—even a year or two, but eventually Mike will present you with an offer you'd be a fool to refuse.' It was impossible to tell anything from his expression, and she gave a helpless shrug. 'It will start all over again. Gradually, maybe. But before you know it, you'll be on stage again, or in front of the cameras—or both,' she ventured quietly. 'You are unequivocally a *star*—whether you want it that way, or not. It takes a very strong person to be able to live with that sort of status.' A slight tremor shook her slim frame. 'I loved you, Laz,' she offered sadly. 'I still do. But it won't work.'

'Damn it, Rachel,' he thrust emotively. 'At least give it a try.'

Her eyes held his, unwavering and incredibly solemn. 'I did. For almost a year. It nearly killed me.'

He seemed to regard her for what seemed an age, and his voice when he spoke was incredibly gentle. 'What we had was special. Something I'd give my life to repossess.' He paused imperceptibly, then continued quietly—'I intend for us to resume our marriage, Rachel. One way or another.'

The mere thought of living with him, loving him, was enough to trip her heartbeat and send it pounding at an alarming rate.

'You can't force me to do anything I don't want to do,' she evinced with seeming conviction, hoping her outward composure revealed nothing of her inner turmoil. 'I think you'd better leave. Millie will be back soon.'

'I was hoping to persuade you to join me for the afternoon.'

'No.' Amazing she could sound so definite. 'What would it prove?'

'I want you with me tonight,' Laz stressed steadily.

'Out there in the front row—or back-stage. I don't care, as long as you're there. Bring your friend—Millie?' His eyebrows slanted in silent affirmation. 'I'll have Mike arrange transport.'

'No.' Last night had been bad enough. The thought of having to sit listening to him sing, and suffer all over again was impossible.

'Rachel—'

'Please leave.' If he didn't go, she'd probably lapse into ignominious tears. She was just barely in control of her emotions now. 'I mean it.'

He looked ready to shake her until every bone in her body rattled, and she glimpsed the visible effort he was making to retain a hold on his temper. 'You refuse to discuss things rationally?'

'There's no point,' she conceded wretchedly. 'We could talk all night and resolve nothing.'

He looked at her long and hard, then seemed to come to a decision, for he moved across the room to the door, pausing to look at her. 'Maybe you're right. *Talking* isn't going to achieve anything.' Reaching out he opened the door, then moved through and closed it quietly behind him.

Rachel hugged her arms together, feeling suddenly cold, despite the warmth of the sun's rays flooding the room through the wide expanse of plate-glass. Moving to the window, she glanced towards the ground with abstracted uninterest, hardly aware of the scene below. A sleek limousine pulled out from the main entrance and eased on to the Esplanade. Laz—chauffeur-driven, and anonymous behind protective smoke-tinted glass.

A shudder raked her slender frame, and suddenly restless she crossed to collect her shoulder bag from her room, intent on leaving the apartment.

Downstairs, she passed in her key at reception and left a message for Millie before making for the beach.

Afterwards she had little sense of time, nor was she aware of the distance she walked along the sandy foreshore, close to the incoming tide. Sometimes a particularly vigorous rush of water swirled over her feet before receding back into the sea. There were several holiday-makers—swimming, surfing, sunbathing, playing handball, talking. The sound of their voices, together with transistorised music barely penetrated Rachel's consciousness.

Seeing Laz again was akin to stirring a smouldering volcano. Foolish to imagine it lay dormant. It was as alive now as it had ever been. If only she hadn't agreed to come to the coast on holiday with Millie. If, if, *if*! Maybe fate, or some celestial power, forced a predestined path that no earthly being could avoid.

It was ages before Rachel finally returned to the apartment. Millie looked relieved, yet anxious, unsure whether to ask even one of the many questions shrieking for an answer.

'Shall we go out to dinner, or would you prefer to order in?'

Rachel sensed her friend's reticence, and felt too mentally enervated to offer an explanation. Part of her wanted to scream out that she'd prefer to pack up and scurry back to the house they shared in Brisbane as fast as humanly possible. Except it wouldn't be beyond Laz's capabilities to hire a private detective to shadow and report her every move. Running away wouldn't solve anything.

'I don't mind,' she murmured, endeavouring to summon a smile. 'You choose.'

'You don't have——'

'Other plans?' she queried wryly. 'No.'

'Oh.'

'Let's go out, shall we?' Her voice was firm, taking the initiative. 'Somewhere ruinously expensive. Tomorrow is our last day, remember?'

'All right.' Millie seemed to brighten considerably. 'I heard of a French-style restaurant a salesgirl in one of the boutiques recommended when I was trying on clothes. Shall we try it?'

Rachel agreed, endeavouring to put any thoughts of Laz on hold—difficult when his forceful image filled her mind and made clear rational thinking almost an impossibility.

'Let me see what you've bought.' Her smile was a concentrated effort. 'You did buy something, I presume?'

The evening was hardly a success, although lack of enjoyment was due to Rachel's inability to focus on anything. Laz was *there*—his face indelibly imprinted in her brain, so that she consciously sought his flesh and blood entity everywhere she looked. It was hardly conducive to unharried digestion, and by the time they returned to the apartment her nerves were in an unenviable state, making her restless and precluding any ability to sleep.

The next day brought little improvement, and she was almost at screaming point when a single red rose was delivered within minutes of them entering the apartment late in the afternoon. There was no need for an accompanying note, and she recognised the slashing signature at a glance. No poetic verbiage, or even a solitary salutation. Just *Laz* on a simple white card.

Damn him—damn, damn *damn*! If she was prone to displays of temper, she could very easily have picked up crockery and thrown it heedlessly on to the ceramic-tiled floor—even taken pleasure in the explosive, crashing china. Instead, she thrust the cellophane-wrapped oblong box out of sight, shut herself in the bathroom and took a leisurely shower, then she dressed for the evening ahead.

An evening cruise of the Nerang River and waterways became a floating party, and she flirted outrageously without the slightest qualm with a rather delightful young man who'd so avidly sought her company all evening. It wasn't very nice of her, or even kind, and the sane sensible part of her deplored it. Letting him down gently when the boat berthed just short of the witching midnight hour took considerable panache, and his angry silence at the evening not ending the way he'd imagined was all too evident. Fortunately, innate good manners forbade any verbal recriminations, and she escaped to her waiting car with Millie, driving away with a burst of speed towards their apartment block, reaching its relative safety feeling relieved and repentant.

Saturday dawned bright and clear, with cloudless blue skies presiding over a translucent ocean and clean tide-washed sand. Packing was a simple matter and achieved with minimum effort.

Checking out of the hotel took only minutes, and Rachel wondered why she felt vaguely uneasy as she drove the Porsche out on to the Esplanade.

Laz's silence over the past forty-eight hours preyed on her mind, and despite the warmth of the day, she shivered. He was biding his time—waiting. She sensed it with the utmost clarity. If he wanted to find her, he could, quite easily. That he had failed to contact her reeked of the fact he had access to her address in Brisbane.

During the hour-long drive she appeared preoccupied, caught up in retrospection to a degree whereby it precluded satisfactory conversation.

The house was airless from being closed up, and Millie followed Rachel's example by flinging wide every window and door. A fine film of dust covered the furniture, and after unpacking they completed numerous household chores before taking a well-earned coffee-break.

'Any plans for tonight?' Millie queried idly, and Rachel shook her head.

'No. I think I'll have a shower, fix a light snack, watch television for an hour or so, then get an early night. Not once during this past week did we get to bed before midnight, and I have to instruct an evening aerobic class as well as my usual afternoon dancing class on Monday.'

'Poor thing. Old age must be catching up with you,' Millie grinned mercilessly, and succeeded in raising a faint smile.

'I'm good at what I do,' she alluded wryly. 'But not sufficiently complacent that I don't realise there are other instructors equally talented waiting to slip into my shoes.'

'The Dance Studio's director is a bit of a tartar, isn't she?'

'Dedicated, and a shrewd business woman,' Rachel corrected, taking her cup into the kitchen where she rinsed and placed it to drain.

At that moment the 'phone rang, and Millie answered, her face wreathed with pleasure, and Rachel overheard her making arrangements to go out.

A quiet evening alone was just what she needed, although later she wasn't so sure. Inevitably her thoughts turned to Laz, evoking a restlessness that both irked and infuriated her.

In bed it was even worse, and she picked up a book and read with resolute determination until sheer exhaustion brought somnolent oblivion just before dawn.

CHAPTER FOUR

BREAKFAST on Monday morning was a far from leisurely meal as both girls endeavoured to regain their pre-holiday routine.

'I'll make the toast,' Rachel declared as Millie gave an audible groan on checking the time.

'I'm going to be late,'

'You won't,' she soothed reassuringly. 'The coffee's made, and the paper has just arrived.' Slotting bread into the toaster, she enquired, 'One piece, or two?'

'Oh—one,' Millie insisted, leafing idly through the newspaper as she sipped her coffee. 'I must have put on a kilo over the past week.'

'Where?' Rachel teased lightly as she buttered, then spread yeast extract on to her own and Millie's toast.

'Hey!' Millie burst out with incredulity. 'Look at this article!'

'What now? Another power strike? Or is it the airlines, this time?'

'Rachel—it's *Laz*.'

A hand clutched hold of her heart, and for a moment she was unable to move. What had happened—an accident? Lord, if he was badly injured, or worse . . . Fear galvanised her limbs into action, and she crossed hurriedly to the table, her eyes darting swiftly over the newsprint.

The photograph of Laz was unmistakable, but it was the bold-face print heading the article that drew her riveted attention.

Laz Delany Announces Reconciliation With Wife And Imminent Retirement in Joint Statement to Press

Beneath the caption, in narrow print and enclosed in quotation—

'Mr and Mrs Delany return to the States this week for an undisclosed period. Asked whether they will settle there, Mr Delany was non-committal, and did not rule out the possibility of residing part of each year in Australia. It is understood he owns property in northern New South Wales.'

Rachel felt the blood drain from her face as the words penetrated and she began to assimilate the consequences. How *dare* he? A cold icy rage began to possess her, all-consuming, so that she hardly registered Millie's hurt expression or caught the reproach in her voice.

'Why didn't you tell me?'

How could I tell you something I didn't even know myself? Rachel longed to hurl emotively.

'I wouldn't have told anyone,' Millie said defensively, and Rachel was on the point of saying something conciliatory when the front doorbell pealed.

Who would call this early? It couldn't be a reporter—damn it, not *yet*, surely?

'I'll see who it is on my way out,' Millie declared, shooting Rachel a faintly perplexed look.

'Millie——' she put out a hand, then let it fall back to her side with helpless resignation as the doorbell rang again, more insistently this time, and Millie hurried out of the room.

Rachel cursed afresh, and draining the last of her coffee she moved out into the hall.

Resting on the small side-table beside the front

door was a single red rose encased in cellophane, and she didn't need to read the accompanying card to know who'd sent it.

Rachel closed her eyes, feeling the increasingly familiar tension knot unenviably inside her stomach, then blind panic sent her rushing into the bedroom, and minutes later every suitcase she possessed lay on the bed, the floor, as she began pulling clothes from the wardrobe, out from drawers, with careless disregard.

A peremptory knock at the front door froze every muscle in her body, and when the brief staccato sound was repeated she slumped against the wall, too enervated to move.

Perhaps if she didn't answer, whoever it was would go away.

A tiny hysterical bubble of laughter escaped from her lips. Don't fool yourself, she derided mentally. Laz was capable of breaking a window— or having his hired bodyguard-cum-chauffeur do it for him.

There was no question of her caller's identity. Laz had calculated every move with diabolical precision. He didn't intend her to slip out of his grasp. Not now—maybe not ever.

Slowly she pulled herself away from the wall and began to walk towards the front door, each step bringing increasing anger.

'Rachel.' The restrained force of his voice seemed to penetrate through to her bones. 'Unlock the door.'

She reached for the handle and turned it, then she stood back. 'There's no need to shout.'

His dark glance probed the tension emanating from her every visible feature, and his mouth tightened fractionally.

'Are you going to ask me in?'

Rachel drew a deep steadying breath, then released it slowly. 'I can't stop you.'

'Such a welcome,' Laz alluded drily, moving past her into the hall, and she shut the door with unnecessary care.

'What did you expect?'

'You've seen a copy of today's newspaper, I gather?'

Her eyes sparked brilliant fire as she threw him a vehement glare. 'Yes!'

The ruthless expression on his compelling features was daunting, and his voice became dangerously soft as he demanded, 'Where's your bedroom?'

'You're joking!'

A slight grimace twisted his lips, and his eyes assumed a taut bleakness. 'You need to pack.'

'I'm not going anywhere with you, Laz.' Amazing she could sound so calm, when inside she was so incensed with rage she felt capable of physical assault.

Reaching out, he took hold of her arm and began leading her down the hall. His grasp was firm, yet even as she attempted to wrench away it tightened into a steel-like band.

Finding her bedroom was simply a matter of elimination, and he surveyed the chaos with speculative interest.

'Running away—*again*, Rachel?' he queried silkily, and her hand flew in a swift arc towards his face.

The explosive sound shocked her, and she stared at the redness darkening his cheek with growning horror, scared and exultant both at the same time.

A muscle tensed at the edge of his jaw. 'I'll let that pass—for now.'

She'd never hit him before—or anyone else, for that matter. It hardly made sense. 'I want a retraction,' she said stiffly, and he shook his head.

'No. The car is waiting outside. When you've finished packing, we leave. Together.'

'And if I refuse?'

His eyes assumed an unaccustomed bleakness. 'I don't think you'll do that.'

'You sound very sure.'

He looked at her in silence, then drawled with calculated indolence, 'Your mother is delighted.'

'My mother?' A hollow feeling manifested itself in the pit of her stomach, and her eyes widened with angry disbelief. 'You've spoken to my *mother*?'

'Early this morning,' Laz responded sardonically. 'She was entitled to hear the news first-hand, rather than read about it in the newspapers, don't you agree?'

'I don't believe you,' Rachel whispered, aghast, hating him for the way he had successfully manipulated her into such an intolerable position.

'It's true. She's expecting us in Sydney for lunch, which . . .' he spared his watch a glance, 'gives us half an hour to get to the airport.'

Icy resolve coursed through her veins. 'You might be able to manhandle me into the car, but the airport will be a different story.'

One eyebrow lifted as his features assumed wry cynicism. 'I don't think so, Rachel,' he accorded drily, and she threw him a wrathful glare.

'Forgive me for forgetting the power of omnipotent wealth.' An hysterical laugh bubbled up in her throat. 'I suppose a chartered jet is sitting on the tarmac, the pilot within call and awaiting our arrival. All formalities smoothly dealt with, Laz?'

'Do you doubt it?'

A feeling of trepidation shivered its way down the length of her spine, leaving in its wake a vague sense of disorientation. 'Doesn't it matter that I don't want to go with you?' There was unbidden appeal in her voice, almost a begging plea that bordered on fear, and she wanted for him to go, yet *stay*, both at the same time. Her face assumed a milky pallor and her eyes became deep haunted pools as he shook his head.

Reaching out he caught hold of her chin, tilting it so she had no option but to look at him. 'The loving never stopped, Rachel.' His eyes darkened with undefinable emotion. 'I doubt it ever will.'

She swallowed the lump that had suddenly risen in her throat. 'What if it has, for me?' It was a puny attempt at bravado, and he knew it.

'You're wasting time,' Laz inferred smoothly, letting her go, and turning towards the remaining partly-packed suitcases he indicated, 'Is this everything?'

'Don't you understand?' she cried emotively. 'I'm not coming with you!'

'You are.' The words held the threat of latent anger, and she watched helplessly as he closed catches and hefted a case beneath each arm, then he bent to pick up another in each hand.

'What about my job, this flat—Millie?' She was so angry she could hardly speak coherently. 'I can't just walk out!'

His dark glance ran the length of her body in swift analytical appraisal. 'You were in the process of doing just that when I arrived. It didn't bother you then.'

'Damn you—*damn* you!'

'I'll have Mike 'phone your employer,' Laz said

hardily. 'As to Millie—you can ring her tonight from Sydney.'

He reached the front door, deposited a case at his feet and released the knob, then he placed all four suitcases at the top of the steps.

Within minutes the driver had retrieved and stowed them in the capacious boot of the waiting vehicle.

'Okay, Rachel,' Laz directed quietly, fixing her with an intent stare. 'Will you walk, or do I carry you?'

'You mean I have a choice?'

'You have precisely one minute to decide.'

There was no doubt he meant it, and she drew a deep steadying breath as she fought against defiance. 'I could cause a scene, have a neighbour call the police——'

'Foolish, when you consider the article in this morning's paper,' he declared wryly, and without warning he slid an arm beneath her knees and lifted her against his chest.

'Put me down!'

'I will. Just as soon as we get to the car.'

'I hate you!'

A faint smile twisted his lips as he reached the lower step. 'Right now, I imagine you do.' He carried her as effortlessly as if she weighed scarcely more than a child, and when he reached the car he put her into the rear seat then moved in beside her and shut the door.

Rachel swung round to face him, her eyes brilliant with angry tears. 'You won't get away with this!'

Laz leaned forward and depressed a switch activating the glass panel between the front and rear seats of the limousine, ensuring privacy without any effort at all.

'Would you like a drink?' He reached for the adjacent cabinet, and she shot him a vehement glare.

'Alcohol—at this hour of the morning?'

One eyebrow rose with sardonic cynicism. 'I was thinking more along the lines of orange juice, mineral water, or coffee.'

If she had anything at all, it would probably choke her, and she shook her head in silent negation.

Laz withdrew a thermos-flask, uncapped it and poured black coffee into a mug, dropped in two cubes of sugar, stirred it, then he sipped the aromatic brew. 'Have you had breakfast?'

Her toast lay uneaten in the kitchen, but no power on earth would let her admit it. 'Do you care?'

His look was cool, assessing, and totally without humour. 'Drink this.' He held out the coffee mug. 'I'll get myself another.' When she didn't make any effort to take it, his eyes narrowed and his voice became silky-smooth. 'Being childish isn't going to achieve anything.'

'What would you suggest, Laz? Compliance—acceptance even, at what amounts to blatant abduction?'

'I prefer to regard it as an exercise that has both our interests at heart,' he drawled, placing the mug into her nerveless fingers. 'Drink it, Rachel. You can have something to eat on the plane.'

Hardly aware of her actions, she lifted the mug and sipped the hot sweet liquid. His silence had an unnerving effect, and after a few minutes she turned and gazed sightlessly out the window, the sun's glare successfully filtered by tinted glass.

At the airport the large vehicle drove through

the security check-point and on to the tarmac,
sliding to a smooth halt beside a small Lear jet.
The chauffeur emerged from behind the wheel to
deal with their luggage, and Rachel saw Mike
move down from the plane as Laz slid out from
the car. Then her door was opened, and Laz took
hold of her hand, helping her to her feet, and his
arm curved round her waist as he urged her up the
few steps into the cabin.

With swift precision it took only minutes for the
plane to reverse out from its bay, taxi on to the
runway, then after receiving clearance it sped
swiftly forward and lifted effortlessly into the air.

Immediately they reached their pre-determined
height, a hostess moved forward, took Laz's order
for toast, boiled egg, orange juice and two coffees
with the sort of deference usually reserved for
royalty. Her curiosity was carefully masked, but
she was in no doubt of the passengers' identity.

Rachel picked at the food when it came, too
much on edge to do it justice, and when the tray
was removed she leaned her head back and closed
her eyes. As an attempt to shut out Laz's forceful
image, it failed dismally, and the images inside her
brain became worse than the reality, so that she let
her eyelids flicker open as she endeavoured to find
something of interest beyond the plane's window.

Almost as if he sensed her disquiet Laz reached
out and caught hold of her hand, threading his
fingers through hers, and after the shock of his
touch, when every nerve flinched at the initial
contact, she let her hand relax, absorbing some of
his strength as it flowed of its own volition,
coursing a familiar path without any need of
direction.

She wanted to cry out against the hunger, the

aching need, that slowly consumed her whole being. Almost as if he recognised the sensation, his fingers tightened measurably, and that only made it harder to bear.

They touched down at Sydney's Kingsford-Smith airport shortly after eleven, and forty minutes later the large hired car with Mike at the wheel pulled into the drive of her mother's suburban Mosman home.

Almost at once the front door opened, and Mrs Devison stood waiting, her face alive with pleasure as Rachel mounted the steps, closely followed by Laz, with Mike bringing up the rear with as much of their luggage as he could carry.

'Rachel!' Her arms enfolded the slim girl close. 'I can't begin to tell you how happy I am for you both.'

What could she say? Blurt out that it wasn't of her making, that Laz had taken matters into his hands and presented her with a *fait accompli*? Instead she merely smiled, murmured something appropriate, and allowed herself to be drawn indoors, aware that her every action merely compounded Laz's declaration.

'I've put you in the guest room,' Mrs Devison indicated as they moved down the hall. 'It's much more comfortable and offers some privacy.'

It was also the only room in the house with an *en suite* bathroom, but not, unless her mother had effected a swift change, a double bed.

'Put your luggage in the spare room for the meantime. You can sort out what you need later and transfer it.'

That, too, made sense.

'I've only brought one with me,' Laz murmured far too close behind Rachel as they reached their room. 'The rest are in Mike's care.'

'Well, I'll leave you to freshen up. Lunch will be ready in half an hour.' With that brightly-issued information Mrs Devison turned and left them.

Rachel surveyed the room with abject interest, noting the two single beds with their quilted polished-cotton spreads, the matching drapes, traditional-styled furniture, pictures on the walls. Beige carpet toned perfectly with the navy and peach floral design utilised with drapes and quilted spreads, and were complemented by matching towels in the adjoining bathroom.

'Nothing to say, Rachel?' Laz drawled, and she turned to face him.

'If I start, I'll never stop.' A faint tremor shook her slim frame as she fought against the anger, the sheer futility of the situation. Her chin lifted fractionally as she met his steady gaze. 'You'd better fill me in with whatever plans you've made. My mother is bound to ask.'

'Wednesday we fly out to Los Angeles,' he revealed slowly, his eyes narrowing as he registered the mixture of emotions chasing each other across her expressive features. 'I'm booked to do a variety special there the following week. I have a new album to cut, two commercials to shoot, and Mike is negotiating a final live performance—we won't know the venue or the date for another week or so.'

She swallowed the lump in her throat with difficulty. 'How long will all that take?' How could she sound so calm? Inside, her nerves were reverbrating and jangling in strident discord.

'Three, maybe four, weeks.'

'And then?'

'We'll holiday somewhere quiet and peaceful, then return to Australia. I have a small farm near

Byron Bay, and I intend spending a few months there—relaxing. Enjoying life—*you*.' His gaze was steady, his expression one of indolent warmth. 'A necessary hiatus to "pause and smell the roses". Then when I'm ready, I'll start working again.'

Her nerve-ends seemed to tauten, stretching close to breaking point. 'What if I choose not to participate in any of it?'

'We've already been through that.'

'Have we?' Her voice rose slightly as latent anger erupted into vengeful rage. 'All I remember is you pulling strings and demanding I dance to your tune!'

'Raise your voice much louder and your mother will imagine we're arguing,' Laz drawled, fixing his attention on her generously curved mouth. 'Kissing you into silence could lead to something more—evocative, and infinitely time-consuming. One eyebrow rose in cynical amusement. 'Who knows? We might miss dinner, as well.'

Rachel felt her eyes fill with shimmering futile tears. 'You—bastard.'

A slight smile twisted the edges of his mouth, but there was no humour evident in his eyes. They were bleak and dangerous—inexorable. 'Will you take the bathroom first, or shall I?'

She looked at him wordlessly, hating him at that moment as she'd never thought it possible to hate anyone. Then she crossed blindly into the bathroom and shut the door.

Sluicing cold water over her face countless times did little to cool her inner rage, and she viewed her stormy features with distaste, forcing herself to relax the tenseness apparent. Smoothing a shaky hand over the length of her hair, she took a deep calming breath, then re-entered the bedroom.

Laz regarded her assessingly, his eyes narrowing faintly as he glimpsed her pale features, and he moved close, taking hold of her chin and lifting it, then his hands slid to cup her face as his mouth lowered over hers with bruising force.

Rachel was too shocked to do anything but stand quiescent for a few timeless seconds, then she began to struggle, balling her hands into fists to flail uselessly against his arms, his ribs—anywhere she could connect.

The pressure of his mouth was relentlessly hard, his tongue invading, pillaging, destructive, until she moaned and silently begged him to desist.

With an angry gesture he released her, and she swayed and would have fallen if he hadn't caught hold of her shoulders.

Her lips felt swollen and sore, the soft inner tissue grazed, and she lowered her head, glad of the swinging curtain of hair that successfully masked her expression.

A husky self-derisive oath caught her ears, and she winced against its explicit, softly-explosive force.

Gentle fingers brushed aside her hair, then lifted her chin, and her lashes swiftly lowered in an attempt to hide the hurt and humiliation.

She felt his fingertips trace the outline of her mouth with featherlightness, probing gently, then she heard his swift intake of breath as he caught sight of the havoc he'd wrought.

'Don't—touch me.' She was breaking up inside, every nerve stretched to its limit, and she had to get away from him, out of this room, while she still held a slim thread of control

Without a further word, she turned and opened the bedroom door, uncaring whether he followed her or not.

Lunch wasn't the easiest of meals, and Rachel pushed the food around her plate, forking small portions of quiche into her mouth along with some salad, then she nibbled without interest on half a crunchy bread roll.

'You're very quiet, darling,' Mrs Devison observed with a faint frown, watching her daughter's efforts to do justice to the meal, and Rachel replaced her fork with apparent regret.

'I ate something on the plane,' she excused, proffering a conciliatory smile.

'My fault,' Laz intervened with urbanity. 'I arrived at the house before Rachel had breakfasted, and afterwards,' he shrugged with perceptible eloquence. 'Food wasn't exactly uppermost in our minds.'

Rachel studiously avoided her mother's gaze, and refused to add comment to Laz's damning words. Ignoring him wasn't possible, but she was darned if she would compound the folly of their so-called reconciliation by acting out a part.

'I gave Mike this number,' Laz indicated, accepting more salad. 'I hope you don't mind?'

'Of course not. He's most welcome to call any time,' Mrs Devison assured.

'It's merely an emergency measure. I'm not expecting to hear from him before tomorrow evening giving a time when the car will collect and transport us to the airport.'

In less than forty-eight hours she would be on a flight she had no wish to take, and the thought filled her with dread. She should tell her mother now, denounce Laz's high-handedness. Yet the words stuck in her throat, unwilling to find voice.

She couldn't *want* to re-board that mad, whirling merry-go-round that was an integral part of Laz's lifestyle, could she? Yet deep inside were the seeds of yearning, nurtured, and clamouring for an existence she was powerless to deny. Five years hadn't erased the memory of his lovemaking, or the wild sweet passion they'd shared, and her body seemed entirely separate from her brain, making her aware just how traitorous were the demands of the flesh.

'I'll make some tea, shall I?' Without waiting for her mother to demur, Rachel stood to her feet and moved into the kitchen.

Surprisingly the afternoon passed very quickly. Laz changed into faded Levi's and a short-sleeved shirt, and prowled round the garden, took it upon himself to mow the lawns, then donned swimming trunks and tirelessly stroked several lengths of the pool before stretching himself out on the lounger to soak up the sun's warmth.

It gave Rachel a necessary respite from his company, and the opportunity to catch up on numerous events with her mother that had occurred and not been relayed in letters.

Rebecca's arrival just before dinner provided some light relief, and her ecstatic greeting coupled with delight over Laz's reappearance was endearing. Bubbling with an effervescent personality, she managed to inveigle several anecdotes about Laz's contemporaries in the recording business, and indeed, monopolised much of the conversation well into the evening until Mrs Devison declared an intention to retire.

'Hell,' Rebecca exclaimed inelegantly, shooting her mother a rueful grin. 'One can always rely on you to be tactful.' She rose to her feet with coltish grace. 'Far be it for me to play gooseberry.' The grin widened into a mischievous smile that encompassed her sister and brother-in-law. 'Good night, you two. I guess I won't see you at breakfast.'

Rachel managed a strangled response, and heard Laz's deep-throated laughter.

'Probably not,' he agreed. 'Don't make plans for tomorrow night, hmn? Rachel and I intend taking you both out to dinner.' Amusement crinkled the fine lines around his eyes. 'Bring the boyfriend of the moment, if you want.'

'You have to be kidding!' Rebecca appeared scandalised. 'I intend basking in reflected glory as everyone recognises you and envies me like mad!'

'I'm sure you'll be doomed to disappointment. My precise whereabouts are a well-kept secret.' A faint edge of cynicism entered his voice. 'As far as the press are aware, I'm still in Brisbane.'

'I suppose venturing into public places can get to be a bit of a hassle,' Rebecca agreed. 'No trendy city restaurant, but somewhere quiet in one of the outer suburbs—right?' She gave a sigh of resignation, and moved towards the door. 'Oh well, at least I'm the only female who can claim you as a brother-in-law.'

The moment Rachel had been dreading had finally arrived. It was well after eleven, and she couldn't think of a single reason to delay going to bed.

'Our turn, don't you agree?'

She looked up and met Laz's partly-veiled gaze, feeling each separate nerve-end stir into vibrant life as his arm lifted from behind her shoulder and his fingers began to thread idly through the length of her hair. It was a gentle action, soothing, and she closed her eyes, too enervated to protest. She didn't want to accept the seducing quality of his touch, but already a heady warmth was coursing through her veins, fanning hidden fires she was loath to acknowledge. Indeed, she would have given anything to be able to ignore the wild leaping of her senses, successfully dampen the longing, the excitement, that made her want to turn towards him and lift her mouth to his.

A tiny groan of despair escaped her throat, and she moved rapidly to her feet, every movement full of agitation as she crossed the lounge and made for the hallway.

By the time she reached the bedroom she was breathing as rapidly as if she'd just completed a strenuous work-out, and she looked around the room wildly, like an imprisoned animal seeking any avenue of escape.

The only place offering temporary sanctuary was the *en suite* bathroom, and she made for it blindly, shutting the door behind her.

It took only seconds to strip off her clothes, wind her hair up beneath a shower-cap, then she turned on the shower and stepped beneath the warm cascading spray of water.

She reached for the soap and began lathering her arms, then her shoulders, and was on the verge of sudsing her breasts when a slight sound at the door alerted her attention.

For a second she froze, then a startled gasp escaped her lips as the tinted-glass shower door slid open and Laz stepped into the stall, his naked muscled flesh a potent virile force.

'You can't——'

'Don't look so shocked,' Laz mocked, reaching for and taking the soap from her hand. 'It isn't as if this is the first time we've shared a shower.'

Then she'd laughed and behaved like a

shameless temptress, taking and allowing liberties, until rapturous desire flared all over again, and Laz had carried her growling like a tormented lion to bed and made slow passionate love that had her begging and moaning like a craven wanton for his possession.

Now she crossed her arms over her breasts and tried to evade the sure path of his hand as it moved the soap across her back, down to her waist and over each gentle curve of her bottom.

When he turned her towards him she began to resist, unable to bear his ministrations a second longer. 'Don't—please——'

'Shut up, Rachel,' he bade dangerously. 'For the love of heaven—just shut up.'

She lifted shaking hands to her face, closing out the sight of him, deliberately blanking her mind to the soft caress of the soap as it travelled her body, then when he'd finished he caught her close against his side and lathered his own frame before rinsing the suds from them both.

Closing the taps, he pushed her gently out of the shower, caught up a towel and wound it round his hips, then he reached for another and began to blot the excess moisture from her skin.

'Was that so terrible?'

There was an edge of mockery apparent in his voice, and she was powerless to move as he shook talc from the array of toiletries standing on the nearby pedestal and began smoothing the perfumed powder over her body.

By the time he'd finished she was a mass of nerves, and it didn't help that he was aware of the effect he was having on her.

'You're doing this deliberately, aren't you?' Rachel demanded in an anguished whisper. 'Taunting, *torturing*—safe in the knowledge that I can't put up too much resistance with my mother and Rebecca sleeping within hearing distance.'

His eyes darkened until they resembled obsidian chips. 'Is that what you think?' He caught hold of her arms, uncaring that his fingers bit into the soft flesh. 'Do you imagine either of them expect us to sleep innocently alone in each bed?'

I'm afraid, don't you understand? she wanted to scream at him. Afraid to let you love me, afraid to let go of the tenuous hold I have on my emotions. Terrified I won't be able to pick up the pieces again if things don't work out.

'Don't tell me you don't want me,' Laz rasped huskily. 'This pulse-beat,' he trailed his fingers across the rapidly throbbing centre at the base of her throat, then travelled down to brush against one tautened peak of her breast before capturing its twin. 'These; even the deep slumbrous dilation of your eyes, give you away.' He drew in a deep harsh breath. 'And me. You think I don't want— *need* you? Sweet Jesus,' he husked emotively, loosening the towel so that it slid from his hips to the floor. 'Do you begin to realise the amount of self-control I've had to exercise all day—all damned evening?' His arms brought her close, so close she could be in no doubt of his arousal.

If only she could lift her arms and pull his head down to hers—bid him blot out the pain, the hurt; physically love him. For a moment she almost did, assuring herself it didn't matter. All she had to do was close her eyes and let Laz sweep her high, lose herself in mindless ecstasy, pleasure him as he was able to pleasure her.

'I don't think I can,' she murmured shakily, lifting her head and willing her eyes to remain steady. 'Not the way you want me. Not yet.'

She could feel the tension build up in him until every muscle became tautly rigid. 'You can't mean that.'

'Can't I?' she queried sadly.

'What would you suggest? A moonlight swim in the pool to work off my frustration, or a cold shower?' His eyes narrowed and became hooded slits. 'Or have your sexual tastes broadened so you now enjoy a firm hand—perhaps even force?'

'*No*. No,' she repeated shakily, horrified and sickened by his allusion.

'Oh, go to bed, for God's sake,' Laz bit out emotively, turning away from her and opening the door.

Rachel slipped past him and crossed to extract a nightgown from a nearby drawer, pulling it over her head with trembling hands, then she slid into bed.

Laz followed within minutes, and she sensed rather than heard him settle beneath the covers, then the lamp between the two beds was extinguished.

She wanted to cry, but no tears would come, and she lay awake staring into the darkness for what seemed an eternity until sheer weariness took over, providing merciful oblivion.

There seemed to be so many images disturbing her subconscious, some shadowy and menacing, so that she fought to be free of them, struggling against innumerable demons bent on captive destruction. At one stage she thought she cried out, and the name she called seemed to echo relentlessly before mysteriously materialising in human form, arms outstretched, welcoming her threshing body, holding it protectively close, so that gradually the fear subsided and became replaced by a bewitching seductive awakening. Passion flared, demanding assuagement, and her dream lover led her slowly, with infinite care, to an ultimate fulfilment so tumultuous she could hardly bear the enchantment to end.

Eventually the many veils of sleep began to lift, and Rachel moved restlessly, reluctant to return to reality. Light filtered through her eyelids, and she opened them slowly, the lashes flickering upwards as she became aware that she was not alone in her bed.

Sapphire blue eyes deepened and grew wide as they caught the slow musing smile, then moved up to meet the dark grey gaze regarding her with an infinite degree of passionate warmth.

'Good morning,' Laz greeted gently, and Rachel looked at him with growing consternation, suddenly aware she was naked. What's more, so was he. Not only that, her skin tingled, and her breasts felt tender, almost swollen.

He lifted a hand and smoothed back her hair, tucking a stray lock behind her ear, then he leant forward and kissed her, gently, tasting the softness of her lips as they parted in surprise.

'Last night,' Rachel whispered tremulously. 'You—we didn't——'

'Make love?' Laz's mouth curved into a warm, intimate smile. 'Yes—beautifully.' His fingers trailed across her cheek, then slid down to the edge of her mouth.

Nightmare had traversed into a dream that had become reality. Had none of the dream been of her subconscious imagination? Isolated sequences provided the answer. Even in sleep her soul had cried out, effectively seeking a consummation without her conscious knowledge.

The profundity of it all eluded her, and she dragged the sheet over her nakedness as she reached for the wristwatch she'd placed on the nearby pedestal, staring at the gold hands with abject dismay.

'It's nine-thirty!'

Laz's teeth showed white. 'Scandalous.'

'What about breakfast—my mother—what will she think?'

He touched a gentle finger to the tip of her nose, his sloping smile full of teasing laughter. 'Your mother was going to drive Rebecca to work, then spend the morning shopping—remember? I distinctly recall her mentioning she wouldn't be back until mid-afternoon,' he mocked lightly. 'I imagine it was a discreet ploy to give us the house to ourselves.'

His face was so close, the strongly-etched bone-structure a mould for an assemblage of muscle and skin that portrayed latent sexuality, lethally enhanced by a sensually-curved mouth above a broad determined chin, expressively liquid grey eyes that could convey incredible intimacy or weary cynicism without seeming effort.

The thought of spending most of the day alone with him awakened the butterflies in her stomach, and she fought to calm her quickened breathing. One thing was sure—she had to get out of this bed, *now*.

'I'll shower and make breakfast,' Rachel declared with a steadiness she was far from feeling, moving away from him, scarcely able to believe he would let her go.

Yet he did, and she caught up a sheet from the adjacent bed, covering her nakedness. Then she selected fresh underwear, cotton trousers and a matching top, and escaped into the bathroom.

The anticipatory fear that he might join her lent incredible speed, and five minutes later she was dressed, her hair brushed and her teeth cleaned.

Laz was extracting Levi's and a shirt from the wardrobe when she re-entered the bedroom, and she studiously avoided his swift gaze, masking the effect his raw masculinity had on her senses by querying uncertainly, 'What would you like to do today?'

Somehow such a loaded question required clarification, and she rushed quickly—'If Mike is available with the car, perhaps we could drive to the Blue Mountains.'

Dark grey eyes flicked over her flustered features, and his expression became vaguely mocking. 'Why not?' He began moving towards the bathroom. 'I'll call him after I've had a shower.'

It became a day that evoked the hidden challenge of presenting an amiable, relaxed front, and at the end of it Rachel felt so emotionally drained and at odds with herself that the thought of dining out filled her with dread. Rebecca and her mother were far too perceptive to be easily fooled, and having to project an affectionate image for several hours would take every ounce of inner strength she possessed.

Later, Rachel could only bless her sister's ebullient ability to provide sparkling witticisms along with a gregarious nature—and more than a glass too many of French champagne. The bubbles slid effortlessly down her throat, eventually entering her bloodstream to set up an odd recklessness. It lent a warm provocativeness to her voice, and added sparkling depth to her brilliant blue eyes.

By tacit agreement they had travelled to the restaurant by taxi, and summoning one for the return trip home was achieved with minimum effort by the management—due, no doubt, to the sizeable bill Laz had settled at the evening's end.

The fresh night air seemed to have an unsteadying effect, and Rachel swayed slightly as she emerged from the taxi, accepting Laz's arm as it curved round her waist.

After a few faltering steps her legs suddenly crumpled. Laughing softly, Laz lifted her into his arms, carrying her effortlessly, and she was conscious of his warm breath fanning her cheek for an instant before she buried her face against his throat.

She remembered bidding her mother and sister good night as they entered the house, then everything took on a hazy glow. She felt strangely weightless, and had a vague recollection of endeavouring to stand as Laz removed her clothes, followed by the startling clarity of his lingering kiss, then she was tucked between the sheets like a child.

Scarcely before she was asleep she was being shaken awake to the sound of Laz's droll voice directing her to rise and shine.

'You're joking,' Rachel groaned, burying her head beneath the pillow in an effort to still the seemingly countless tiny hammers beating a relentless tattoo inside her head.

'Tomato juice, pepper, and a dash of tabasco,' he drawled, removing the pillow and hauling her into a sitting position.

'Ugh! Black coffee and a couple of aspirin will do just fine,' she muttered, pushing his hand away.

'This first, hmn,' he persisted, placing the glass

to her lips and tilting it. 'Then a shower, and after you're dressed, you get the coffee.'

'Don't be so damned bossy.' She wished he would go away and leave her to suffer alone.

'Mike will be here in less than an hour to take us to the airport.' He watched the play of emotions chase across her expressive features, and a muscle tensed along his jaw. 'I thought that might instil the need for action.'

Oh *God*! 'I don't think I can make it.' At this precise moment she doubted she could stand, let alone walk.

'That bad, hmn?' He sounded grimly amused and hatefully cynical. 'Never mind, you can sleep all the way to Los Angeles.'

She winced, her brow furrowing in pain. 'Don't shout.'

'You want me to put you beneath the shower, then dress you?'

'The hell you will.' She turned back the covers, then slid to her feet, her eyes alive with defiance. 'And I won't drink that ghastly concoction, either!'

His deep-throated laughter was the living end, and she pushed past him on her way to the *en suite* bathroom.

It was perhaps as well she didn't have time to think, for if she'd had a chance to reflect she probably would have had a last-minute attack of jitters and refused point-blank to go.

As it was, Mike arrived early, their combined luggage was stowed in the capacious boot, then Laz handed her into the luxurious rear, closely followed by Mrs Devison and Rebecca, then he slid into the front seat beside his manager.

The drive to the airport seemed far too short,

and in a flurry of protocol they were whisked through Customs after a hurried, tearful farewell, then accorded V.I.P. treatment and escorted directly into the business section of the giant Boeing 747 with only minutes to spare before take-off.

The smooth precision of it all, coupled with the fact that the entire upper lounge was taken over by Laz's entourage, merely heightened Rachel's awareness of what lay ahead. Without doubt there were two hired bodyguards, one seated at the base of the curved stairs, one at the top, to ensure no curious passengers elected to pursue their curiosity and intrude.

She was supremely conscious of Laz sitting close beside her, the swift powerful thrust of engines as the huge jet taxied down the runway and ascended high into the clouds, and she closed her eyes in an attempt to shut out his forceful image.

CHAPTER FIVE

A HAND touched her shoulder briefly, then fingers brushed against her cheek, and Rachel opened her eyes slowly, momentarily startled until she became aware of her surroundings, the man at her side.

'The hostess is about to serve lunch,' Laz intimated quietly, his gaze becoming faintly hooded as she shook her head.

'I don't want anything.'

'Accept the tray, and eat something,' he warned softly. 'You'll feel better, then you can sleep.'

How long had they been in the air? Half an hour? An hour? A quick glance at her watch revealed it to be the latter. 'I *was* asleep,' she reminded with slight sarcasm, and the edges of his mouth twisted into a wry smile.

'You missed breakfast, remember?'

'Such solicitude over my welfare,' she mocked, tempering it with a sweet smile as the hostess leaned across and placed a tray in position.

Laz shot her a penetrating glance, then picked up his cutlery and cut into the succulent-looking meat on his plate.

Rachel followed suit, unwilling to admit that he was right. The food did help, despite the fact she didn't finish it all, and after black coffee she felt distinctly human again.

'Congratulations,' she offered when both trays had been removed.

One eyebrow rose slightly in quizzical query, and she enlightened with a trace of mockery.

'On achieving your objective. Me—on this plane.' She met his gaze unflinchingly. 'Is that why you kept filling my glass with champagne last night? Knowing damn well I'd pass out, then feel so terrible this morning I'd offer the least possible resistance?'

'Would you believe I had Mike organise the Australian tour with that specific purpose in mind?'

She seemed to stop breathing, and after an infinitesimal space of time the words tumbled out. 'You had no idea where to find me, and my mother wouldn't have——'

'Told me?' he drawled, his expression becoming darkly cynical. 'It wasn't necessary.'

'What do you mean?' Her mind began to whirl out of control at his implication.

'You were very careful to cover your tracks.' He paused deliberately, watching the play of emotions over her expressive features. 'So careful it took several months to trace you. Fortunately, perhaps,' he alluded with sardonic grimness. 'By then I'd traversed from rage to resignation. There was nothing I could do but put our marriage on hold until such time as existing contracts were fulfilled.'

'You knew where I was—all the time?'

'Do you want a list?' Laz parried with formidable detachment. 'Adelaide, Melbourne, Perth, Darwin, Cairns, Townsville, Rockhampton, Brisbane. You want addresses as verification?'

The thought that her every action had been carefully watched, recorded and despatched made her ill.

'Imagine my surprise,' he continued cynically. 'When Mike reported seeing you among the audience at the Twin Towns Club at Tweed Heads a few days before I intended instigating a confrontation.'

'So you knew I was holidaying on the Coast with Millie?'

His brief nod was damning, and she slumped back in her seat feeling positively sickened.

The efforts she'd made to ensure an elusive anonymity these past few years seemed horribly ironic.

'What would you have done if I'd become involved with another man?' The desire to wound was uppermost, and she enjoyed the faint flaring of his nostrils, the tightness of his mouth.

'There's no point in discussing something that didn't happen.'

'How can you know for sure?' A taunting quality entered her voice. 'Your inestimable trench-coated private detective may have maintained enviable vigilance, but he could hardly have possessed x-ray eyes!'

'You've been watching too much television.'

'Oh, of course,' she acceded with sarcasm. 'One could hardly be expected to skulk around in a trench-coat in the tropics.'

'Don't act the shrew,' he drawled. 'It doesn't suit you.'

She had to get away from him, if only temporarily, and she rose to her feet, waiting while he moved out into the aisle so that she could pass him.

Tidying her hair and repairing her make-up utilised only a few minutes, but she deliberately took longer than necessary in an effort to regain her composure. Her mirrored image revealed none of the inner tension, and only the keenest gaze could determine the falseness of her smile as she made her way back to her seat.

She even managed a friendly greeting as she passed Mike and Brad, then Zeke and Pete, and her smile was nothing less than brilliant as she encountered Simi's speculative gaze.

Resuming her seat, Rachel leaned back and closed her eyes in a determined effort to ignore her inimical husband, the consequences their reconciliation would have, and worse and more immediate—how she would weather being thrust into the public eye again.

During the sixteen-hour flight she alternatively dozed, leafed through magazines, pretended intense interest in a thick historical saga paperback Rebecca had thrust into her bag just prior to departure, or plugged in the headset provided. Anything to keep verbal contact with Laz to a minimum.

Their arrival at Los Angeles International airport was dealt with smooth efficiency, despite the inevitability of flashing cameras aimed in their direction and persistent questioning from a few zealous reporters.

'Smile, sweetheart,' Laz directed in a deceptively soft undertone as he caught her close in against his side, and she complied with dazzling obedience.

'Good enough, *darling*?'

Grey eyes darkened, and his teeth gleamed white as his head lowered. 'Oh—*stunning*.'

His kiss was deliberate, she knew, and lingered just long enough to appear totally convincing, then he laughingly refused any further photographs, and Rachel heard Mike reveal he'd arrange a press conference within the next few days, thus providing satisfaction and allowing them uncluttered passage to an imposing pair of limousines parked immediately out front.

'Where to, Laz?' Rachel queried as the large vehicle swept away from the kerb and joined the flow of traffic. 'Hotel, apartment? Or have you acquired a home in prestigious Beverly Hills?' She was being facetious, and didn't care. 'Even a Malibu beachhouse? That's an elevated status symbol, I believe.' Tinted glass windows ensured total privacy from outside eyes, and panelled glass between front and rear compartments prevented them being overheard.

Laz directed her a long cool glance. 'I was never into status symbols.'

'Five years is a long time. You could have changed.'

'I own a home,' he revealed unemotionally. 'A retreat, set high in the hills above Los Angeles.'

She held his gaze without flinching. 'I'm suitably impressed.'

His mouth twisted into a wry smile. 'It affords me essential privacy.'

'Complete with every luxury, and safeguarded by an elaborate highly-sophisticated security system. Carefully concealed, of course,' Rachel added cynically, and his eyes narrowed fractionally.

'It's a necessary precaution.'

'Oh, I'm sure it is,' she agreed blandly. 'One is made increasingly aware of the almost paranoiac need for multi-millionaire *stars* to be protected in their million-dollar residences.'

'Bitch,' he accorded softly, reaching out to curl his fingers beneath the swathe of hair at her nape, tugging mercilessly until he brought her face within inches of his own.

'Don't you *dare*!' Rachel hissed, hating the way her senses leapt at the threat of his lowering mouth.

His quick indrawn breath and the faint narrowing of his eyes warned of limited patience, and she twisted her head in an effort to evade that plundering invasion, wincing as the pressure on her tender scalp increased with painful intensity.

The next instant she was dragged effortlessly across the seat to half-sit, half-lie against him, and even as she began to protest it was stilled beneath the hungry ravaging possession of his mouth.

As a punishment it was very effective, and she was conscious of the solid wall of his muscular chest, the hardness of his hands as they held her. Worse, the ruthless force of his lips as they heartlessly crushed hers.

Any attempt to struggle proved fruitless, and a silent groan of self-defeat rose in her throat as she relaxed her jaw and allowed him entry. Frustrated angry tears clouded her vision and she clenched her lids tightly shut in an effort to prevent them spilling over.

Futility, humiliation, *pain*, culminated together to combine with a deep inner rage, and she brought her teeth together in damnable revenge.

His fierce husky oath was viciously explicit, and the icy anger evident in his eyes sent every muscle in her body rigid with fear.

Time seemed to pause in explosive suspension as her eyes became locked with his, dilating, expressive and unblinking.

It was as if she'd wanted to hurt him for all the suffering of five years ago, the emptiness in between, and the sheer futility of being forced to experience it all over again. Yet part of her recognised *his* anger; with her, as well as himself, the circumstances that were beyond their control—or had been, up until now.

She wasn't capable of uttering a word, and the silence between them lengthened until it gained frightening proportion, broken only by the slight whisper of the vehicle's powerful engine as it climbed ever higher through the hills.

Rachel moved, shifting away to resume her seat, and she stared sightlessly out the tinted window until the limousine paused before electronically-controlled gates, then it swept up a wide curving drive to halt outside an unpretentious but large home set well back from the road and almost totally obscured by trees.

The door beside her opened, and she slid out to stand uncertainly on the paved courtyard, conscious of the chauffeur's presence as Laz crossed round to her side.

Even as she hesitated the front door opened and a large loose-limbed man moved forward to greet them.

'Laz—Rachel.' He seemed in no doubt as to her identity, and she felt the slight warning pressure as Laz's fingers closed over her arm.

'My caretaker, Hank. He and his wife, Hannah, look after the place for me.' His smile seemed relaxed and friendly. 'When I'm home, Hannah sees to it that I'm well-fed.'

Somehow she was indoors, vaguely aware of tiled floors, a wide entrance from which various doors led, and a curved staircase set well back against a magnificent panel of stained glass.

'I'll see to the baggage,' Hank inferred easily. 'I expect you'd both prefer to shower and change.'

It had been a long flight, and despite snatching a few hours' sleep on the plane, Rachel felt tired. Under normal circumstances she would have looked forward to exploring the house, wandering at will through the many rooms. Now all she wanted was to be left alone.

'Tell Hannah we'll be down in an hour for lunch,' Laz indicated, moving towards the staircase. 'Just something light. Rachel? Any preferences?'

She looked up quickly and glimpsed the inscrutable expression in his eyes. The last thing she felt like was food. Her body seemed listless and weary, crying out for a bed in which to relax and hopefully *sleep*. Yet it was just midday.

'A sandwich will be fine.'

Like a docile child she walked upstairs, along the length of the hall to a large bedroom whose windows overlooked the magnificent vista of valley and sky.

Rachel barely registered the muted shades of beige, honey and cream, with splashes of colour emanating from impressionist prints on the walls.

It wasn't a man's bedroom, nor was it entirely feminine—merely a pleasing combination that exuded a restful air.

She gave a faint start as Laz touched a control panel and the drapes swished slowly closed.

'You look tired.'

Her head had begun to throb, and she lifted a hand to an aching temple. 'Yes.'

'Go and have your shower,' he bade quietly.

'My luggage——'

'Will be here by the time you're ready to change.' When she would have hesitated, he took her arm and led her towards an adjoining bathroom, pushed her firmly inside, then closed the door.

Left alone, Rachel mechanically began to divest her clothes, then she stepped beneath the cascading water, enjoying its relaxing warmth for several minutes before reaching for the soap.

It was ten minutes before she emerged and towelled herself dry, then fastening the towel sarong-fashion about her slim form she opened the door to find the bedroom empty.

As promised, all her suitcases stood beside the bed, and she quickly unpacked her toiletries, fresh underwear. Encountering a silk wrap she quickly slipped it on, then looked enviously at the large bed.

Dare she? Without thought she turned back the coverlet and was about to slide between the sheets when Laz entered the room.

He had obviously showered, and with a towel hitched carelessly about his hips he looked dynamically male.

Her eyes widened slightly at the sight of so much tanned muscled flesh, the taut ribcage, the rough hairs matting his chest, then arrowing down to his navel. His hair curled damply about his head, and although she'd seen him like this countless times in the past, there was something almost animalistic about his stance that held her motionless in mesmerised fascination.

'Have I suddenly grown horns?' A faint quirk of humour lifted the edges of his mouth, and one eyebrow rose in cynical amusement.

'Another set, do you mean?'

'Still sore at me?'

'Specifically, or in general?' she parried evenly, averting her eyes as he moved close.

'Jet-lag has begun to take its toll, hmn?' He took hold of her chin between thumb and forefinger, lifting it so she had little option but to look at him.

She deliberately kept her lashes lowered, hating

the tell-tale pulse that began to beat rapidly in the hollow at the base of her throat.

'If you don't mind, I'll take a nap.' The words came out in a nervous flutter, and she swallowed, *feeling* the intensity of his scrutiny to such a degree she could hardly breathe.

'Headache?'

'Yes, damn you!'

'Oh, Rachel,' he mocked lightly. 'That bad?' His fingers brushed her cheek, then probed her left temple. 'There?'

Their caressing quality was almost her undoing, and she moved restlessly, willing her body not to respond to his flagrant seduction. If he stayed much longer, there would be no hiding the way she hungered for him. 'An hour's sleep will get rid of it.'

'With, or without me?'

Her eyes flew wide at the humorous implication in his voice, and she attempted to wrench out of his grasp. 'Damned egotist! *Without you.*'

'Such vehemence,' he mocked gently, cupping her face with both hands and letting his thumbs trace lightly over each cheekbone. 'I've spent five years remembering every facet of our lovemaking. Each separate pulse-beat, the way your lashes sweep down and quiver when you're trying to hide your emotions, how you swallow convulsively when you want my kiss. The nervous worrying of your lower lip with your teeth, the way your eyes deepen into dark pools of sapphire. You want me to go on?'

Was she so transparent? It was scary to think another person knew her so intimately—even more intimately than she knew herself.

'Stop trying to erect barriers, Rachel,' Laz bade

gently. 'You're mine. You always were—always will be.'

'Am I?' She felt shaky, unequipped to cope with him. He had always swamped her, and that was when she was sure of him, of herself. Now it was a hundred times worse.

His warm breath fanned her forehead, teasing the soft tendrils of hair at her temple. 'You know it.'

Did she? Perhaps he was right. Maybe she was erecting barriers. Yesterday was gone, regrets or none. Nothing they could do or say could change the past.

'I'm tired,' she whispered in momentary defeat, and felt his hands slip down past her shoulders to the back of her waist as he curved her against him.

'I know.'

Rachel sensed him move, then he slid into bed with her gathered in his arms, and she began to protest.

'Shh—just lie still. I'm not going to do anything you don't want me to do.'

'Laz——'

His mouth touched hers, tracing its outline with feather-lightness, lingering at the edge before brushing back to the other side, then moving to the centre of her lower lip and teasing back its soft fullness.

Slowly, and with infinite care, he let his lips trail along the edge of her jaw to her cheekbone, across to a closed eyelid, down the length of her nose, the slight dimple in her right cheek, then across to an earlobe and down the pulsing cord at her neck.

Almost of their own volition her fingers moved to thread themselves through his hair, their touch trembling slightly as they encompassed the warmth of his skin, the firm sculptured bone structure outlining his forehead, cheekbone and jaw. Like a blind person she let her fingers braille his face, familiarising themselves with every crevice and hollow, feeling new depths in age lines that hadn't been quite so evident five years before.

In turn, his lips brushed down to the valley between her breasts, slipping aside the silken folds of her wrap, dispensing with it unhurriedly before beginning what became a supplication of every inch of her subtly scented skin, all the hollows, the soft inner moistness that led to the central core of her being, giving pleasure until she begged him to stop.

Then he moved above her, lowering himself gently into her welcoming embrace, and their loving assumed an elusive meshing of alchemy and witching enchantment that was theirs alone. A merging of two spirits so attuned in unison, their fusion seemed to transcend beyond the realms of reality.

Returning from that illusory plateau was a slow warm process, as they gradually relinquished their hole on sensory sensuality, drifting slowly to sleep, wrapped in each other's arms.

When Rachel woke it was dark, and for a few timeless seconds she had no knowledge of where she was, then memory surfaced with the weight of a leg laying across her own, an arm curved about her waist, and the steady heartbeat close beneath her head.

She drew in a deep breath, then slowly expelled it as the faint stirrings of angry resignation began to surface. Damn Laz. Damn her own traitorous emotions. She didn't want to *feel* like this, to become so caught up with him she couldn't even think straight.

'What's going on inside that head of yours, hmn?' Laz's deep voice murmured huskily, and she almost stopped breathing with the shock of discovering he was awake.

'What time it it?'

'God knows,' he disclaimed. 'Does it matter?'

Her stomach rumbled in protest, her body-clock attuned to another timespan. 'I'm hungry.'

'So am I,' he inclined lazily, rolling on to his side, one hand moving to close possessively over her breast.

'Food—we missed lunch,' she reminded wryly.

'And dinner.'

He sounded amused, and she threw him a baleful glare that went unnoticed in the darkness. Tossing aside the bedcovers she slid to her feet, and heard a faint click as Laz snapped on the bedlamp.

'Where do you think you're going?' he drawled.

There was something almost paganistic about the sight of the rumpled bedsheets partly covering his powerfully-muscled frame. His hair was ruffled, his eyes dark with lambent warmth, and the sensual curve of his mouth brought forth a flood of tremulous sensation as her traitorous body began an unbidden response.

A lump rose in her throat, and she swallowed convulsively. To stand here was madness, and she determinedly caught up her discarded robe and slipped it on.

'The kitchen,' Rachel informed equably.

'Ah, you're going to display some of your wifely virtues and fix us a snack.' He gaze became openly mocking, and she cast him a cool blue glance.

'If you want to eat, you'll have to accompany me downstairs.'

Dark eyes grew warm with silent laughter. 'Pity,' Laz murmured lazily. 'I rather fancy a picnic in bed. It could end up being fun.'

Ignoring him, she turned and left the room, and by the time she reached the stairs he was right behind her, a dark blue towelling-robe belted at his waist.

'Hannah has probably left something for us in the refrigerator,' he murmured quietly as they reached the lower floor, and she followed him to a large well-equipped kitchen at the rear of the house.

A small table was set for two covered with an organza tablecloth, and she watched as he crossed to remove a note anchored prominently on a cork noticeboard next to the oven.

'Hmm,' Laz mused, scanning it quickly. 'There's a casserole which will take only a few minutes to heat in the microwave. And Mike rang. He's arranged a press conference for us at ten tomorrow morning—today,' he corrected a trifle wryly.

'*Us?*'

His dark glance seemed to sear through to her very soul. 'You're sitting in with me,' he declared silkily, and she shook her head in silent negation. '*Yes*, Rachel.'

'Fantastic,' she muttered stiltedly. 'I'm only in the country a few hours, and you throw me to the wolves.'

His gaze was remarkably steady. 'I'll be there.'

'Hah,' she discounted with deliberate sarcasm, and her eyes sparked with anger.

'Make some coffee,' he directed hardily. 'While I see to the casserole.'

Minutes later Laz apportioned generous servings on to each plate, then carried them to the table. 'Come and eat.' His voice held a trace of mockery, and without a word she slid into the chair opposite and picked up her fork.

Throughout the meal she hardly ventured a word, and afterwards she rinsed the few plates they'd used and placed them in the dishwasher.

'What now?' she asked civilly. 'I don't feel like going back to bed.'

Laz directed her a dark slanting glance, and his mouth assumed a cynical twist. 'Don't act the martyr, Rachel,' he taunted softly. 'You wanted me as badly as I needed you.'

'A slaking of physical lust,' she retaliated swiftly, and he placed his fingers over her lips, his eyes darkening with anger.

'You think so?' One eyebrow rose in sardonic query. 'I retain a vivid recollection of how beautiful it was—for both of us.'

She swallowed the lump that had suddenly risen in her throat, and for some reason she was unable to tear her eyes away from his. 'You're forcing me to take an encore on our short-lived marriage,' she began wretchedly, her eyes begging him to understand. 'I don't want to have to go through it all again—the parties, the incredible bitchiness and one-up-manship, the terrible—"oh, you look divine, darling" platitudes that get handed out on every occasion. I don't want to have to plan every move we make whenever we venture out together in public.' Her eyes sparked with angry fire, then became incredibly sad. 'I wasn't equipped to deal with it six years ago. I'm not sure I can now.'

Hands closed over her shoulders, pulling her close, and she rested her head against his chest, feeling overwhelmingly helpless against forces over which she had little or no control.

'I have hundreds of thousands of fans out there,' Laz said quietly. 'I want them to know I regard you as something special in my life. One joint press release, then I'll handle anything else on my own.'

His lips brushed her temple, then slid down to capture her mouth in a kiss that was sweet and gentle.

'Let's take a shower,' he suggested softly. 'By then it will be almost dawn, and you can 'phone your mother to let her know we've arrived safely.'

CHAPTER SIX

RACHEL had forgotten what it was like to suffer the relentless barrage of flashbulbs, the persistent questions voiced by heartless newshounds intent on getting good copy for their respective news-papers and magazines.

She'd deliberately chosen fashionable attire with utmost care, given considerable time ensuring her make-up was nothing less than perfect, and it said much for her expertise that the make-up artist had merely touched a shade more blusher to her cheeks, and deepened the colour of her lipstick.

Laz looked the epitome of sophistication, his grooming immaculate, and attired in hip-hugging dark suede trousers, a casual white shirt left unbuttoned at the neck, and matching dark jacket, he projected a latent sexuality that was, electrify-ing.

Like bullets from a machine-gun, the questions shot forth without any pretence of observing the conventional niceties.

'Many actors have announced their retirement, only to emerge back on to the television scene. You enjoyed a very successful few seasons with a top-rated show. Why refuse to take up your option?'

'Is it true the studio has doubled your salary and thrown in a percentage of the gross in an effort to get you back for another season?'

'Will you remain in Los Angeles?'

'Your name has been linked with several actresses. Melissa Kiernan, your co-star, in particular. You've been seen dining together, and she accompanied you to last year's Emmy and Grammy Awards.'

Laz answered them with commendable ease, even managing to inject some humour into what Rachel could only term a bizarre situation.

'Any television series, no matter how successful, possesses a certain life-span. Along with the producers, I felt we'd explored every credible angle. Extending it for another season would have damaged the quality and brought a drop in ratings. My *retirement* as such, means no more tours, no further television series. I intend to spend more time writing music.'

'Your wife is Australian,' a woman reporter pursued. 'Will you live there, and commute to the States?'

'What of Melissa Kiernan? Or would you prefer not to comment for obvious reasons?'

Laz leaned back in his seat, displaying urbane equanimity. 'I intend spending some time in the States—although the length and frequency of such visits are impossible to forecast.' A broad smile broke his mouth, and his teeth showed strong and white. 'I do possess a few friends in this town. Melissa happens to be one of them.'

Rachel experienced a shaft of incredible pain, identifiable as jealousy in its severest form. It made her want to lash out; hurt as she was being hurt; publicly, and without a shred of compassion by gossip-hunting piranhas who possessed no emotions of their own and cared even less for hers. Perhaps that's what they wanted—to capture visually on celluloid a sense of vulnerability and indecision that would be lacking in the written word.

'Relax,' Laz had advised just prior to the press

conference. 'All you have to do is sit there, look beautiful, and smile. I'll do all the talking.'

'And you, Mrs Delany,' one hard-faced reporter breasted with daring audacity. 'Having absented yourself in Australia for the past five years, one can only imagine you possess similar—friends?'

The emphasis was a little too noticeable not to be deliberate, and Rachel felt a familiar surge of anger rise to the surface. Summoning a singularly sweet smile she met the woman's gaze and gently ventured an answer.

'Australia *is* my home-country. As well as family, I have a number of life-long friends there.' She let her smile widen, deliberately cultivating a measure of captivating warmth, even a degree of mischievousness as she glanced towards the man at her side. 'I think countless women will agree that Laz would be a hard act for any man to follow.'

There was a general burst of laughing agreement, and Laz slanted her an amused glance tinged with rueful cynicism.

'Five years is a long time to be apart,' the same reporter persisted. 'Did you leave because of unaccustomed pressures?'

Rachel met the woman's stare with cool appraisal. 'I'm sure you don't expect me to answer that.'

'What prompted a reconciliation?'

My God, the woman deserved an 'A' for sheer dogged perseverance!

'There was never any question of Rachel and I not resuming our marriage,' Laz intervened smoothly. 'Merely *when*.'

'One presumes you will start a family?' Another reporter prompted, disregarding Rachel entirely.

'How many children would you like to have?'

'Two.' Laz leaned forward and caught hold of Rachel's hand, lifting it, then he carried it to his lips, his gaze warm and incredibly intimate. 'However, the ultimate decision will rest with my wife.'

'You have no desire for a career, Mrs Delany?'

How was she supposed to respond to that? Either way would be equally damning! 'I guess it depends how you define the word "career".'

'You were a dancer, I believe.' The reporter, a young man, ventured further, 'In which specific area? Ballet? Jazz?'

'I thought this was to be Laz's press conference,' she fielded lightly. 'Not mine.'

'What plans do you have for the following few weeks, Mr Delany?'

'I'm performing at a charity special next Saturday,' Laz informed evenly. 'My manager is negotiating a final live performance, and the date and venue will be announced just as soon as arrangements have been confirmed.' He effected a negligible shrug. 'I have two commercials to film, an album to cut.'

'That's it?'

'Then I intend taking a long overdue holiday.'

'A second honeymoon?'

Laz slid a warm glance towards Rachel. 'I guess you could call it that.'

Mike, who until now had remained quietly in the background, stepped forward, his presence quietly purposeful as he adroitly brought the conference to a close, and Rachel followed Laz's lead by standing to her feet and allowing him to shepherd her from the room.

'Thank heavens that's over!'

They were in the corridor, walking towards the lift, and flanked on each side by Brad and Zeke.

'It wasn't too bad,' Laz acknowledged with elusive cynicism, and the glance he threw her held a measure of amusement. 'You managed very well.'

'Thanks,' she accorded uncharitably. 'It was on the tip of my tongue to disagree with everything and cause a furore.'

The elevator doors slid open and they stepped inside, riding the plushly-fitted carriage down to the ground floor.

'Don't act independent, hmn?' Laz warned. 'The car's out front. Go with Zeke if I get waylaid—okay?'

Rachel effected a mock-salute. 'Yessir.'

'Don't be so darned sassy,' he bit out as the lift whispered to a halt, and she threw him a stunning smile.

'Do I look suitably ecstatic?'

He didn't reply. Instead he threw her a narrowed glance then transferred his attention to the lobby, calculating the number of waiting fans as he summoned an indolent smile, pausing as the first of the group reached him, autograph book and pen at the ready.

Rachel could only admire his calm unruffled composure as he laughingly took the proffered book.

'Okay, honey. What's your name?'

'Michelle,' the attractive blonde informed breathlessly.

Rachel felt the firm touch of a hand on her arm, and she caught Zeke's silent command, knowing she should go, yet wanting out of a perverse sense of curiosity to stay.

'Rachel.' There was a hint of underlying steel in Zeke's voice, an urgency she was unable to assimilate.

'Laz Delany. *Hey*, that guy's *Laz Delany*!'

Somehow the number of girls increased twofold as several joined the original cluster, and a few near the rear began to jostle and push, knowing it was extremely unlikely their idol would stay more than ten minutes or so.

Brad acted as an effective buffer, requesting a semblance of order and getting it, albeit with great reluctance and several disgruntled voices proclaiming they'd been waiting for hours.

'Let's hit the front entrance, *pronto*,' Zeke bade brusquely. 'I don't want to act heavy—'

Rachel didn't say so much as a word as she allowed him to lead her quickly towards the waiting vehicle, and the instant she was seated, he moved quickly back indoors.

Even from this distance she felt sickened by the scene, alarmed, even frightened. It was only an incident, and a minor one, but it made her aware how important was the precision and planning involved that accompanied Laz wherever he happened to go.

Fifteen minutes—fifteen anxiety-ridden minutes later, the driver switched on the car's ignition, and Rachel kept her eyes riveted on the revolving glass doors leading out from the lobby.

Then Laz's tall figure emerged, joined immediately by Brad and Zeke. Seconds later they were in the car, and they hardly closed the doors than the vehicle surged forward, its tyres squealing in protest as the driver concentrated on getting away from the hotel entrance and into the stream of traffic.

Rachel was supremely conscious of Laz sitting close beside her, the hard muscular length of his thigh touching her own, the faint aroma of his aftershave, but most of all the air of leashed tension evident.

She was dimly aware of Zeke's voice, then the deeper rejoinder from Brad, but she didn't register their conversation. Such was her preoccupation she didn't even object when long lean fingers threaded themselves through her own.

'Mike and Pete are following us back to the house. Simi, too,' Laz informed her dispassionately. 'Business. It'll take a few hours. Do you mind?'

What if she did? Would it matter

She didn't trust herself to speak, merely nodded her head in acquiescence, and when the car pulled to a halt outside the large palatial home she slipped quietly indoors ahead of the men.

Upstairs she made for the bedroom, and once there she walked up and down, unconsciously pacing, feeling vaguely disorientated and oddly restless.

Staying in the house didn't appeal, but browsing among some of the exclusive shops and boutiques would provide hours of pleasure.

The decision made, she picked up her bag, checked she had sufficient money, then hurried from the room.

Downstairs she penned a quick note and propped it against the elegant chiffonier in the entrance foyer.

The garage was situated at the side of the house, and Rachel eyed the three cars rather dubiously, dismissing at once the silver Rolls Royce. It was a clear choice between a Range Rover or a metallic-blue Mercedes sports sedan.

The Mercedes was unlocked with the keys stowed in the glove-box, along with a remote-control device to operate the front gates.

A few minutes later she breathed a sigh of relief as the car cleared the driveway, and she swung the wheel, heading towards fashionable Bel Air.

Re-familiarising herself with left-hand drive demanded concentration, and it was something of a relief to ease the sleek sports car into a parking space without incident.

An hour later, having eaten in a charming restaurant, she began wandering at will, exploring the numerous boutiques with no real intention of purchasing anything.

However the temptation was too much to resist, and she bought a pair of shoes, a blouse, and an exquisite silk scarf, then enjoyed a leisurely coffee before making her way back to the car.

A glance at her watch revealed she'd been away for more than three hours, and as she drew closer to home she wondered if her absence had been noticed.

Reaching the tree-lined street she drove through the electronically-controlled gates, then brought the car to a halt in its original position inside the garage.

Scarcely had she emerged from behind the wheel than two figures converged, and she forced a careless smile as she extracted her purchases from the passenger seat. Hank, *Laz*—the latter looking coldly furious.

'Where the *hell* have you been?'

'Shopping,' Rachel informed with an attempt at lightness, and Laz threw his retort bleakly.

'Alone?'

'Sorry,' she said sweetly, not sorry at all. 'I

didn't realise I had to ask permission.' A brilliant
smile curved her lips as she gazed at her forceful
husband. 'If you didn't want me to drive one of
your cars, you had only to say so.'

'God,' Laz bit out hardily. 'I could wring your
blasted neck.'

'Language, darling,' she reproved, clicking her
tongue. 'Whatever will Hank think?'

'Precisely the same as I do,' he said heavily.
'That I'm exercising remarkable restraint.'

'I left a note.'

'Don't sound so damned sanctimonious.'

'Can't we discuss this civilly, without it
digressing into a slanging match?' She harboured a
full measure of resentment, and if he wanted a
fight, he'd darned well get one!

'You should have told me you wanted to go out.
I'd have had—'

'Someone drive me,' she finished wryly, her eyes
flashing angrily. 'I needed to be alone, Laz.
Somewhere I could be *me*, without being taken
there in a chauffeured limousine and a bodyguard
shadowing my every move.' She met his narrowed
gaze and held it with remarkable clarity. 'There
was no fear of me getting lost. I spent a year in
Los Angeles, remember?'

'Five years ago,' Laz declared brusquely. 'Times
change. So do people.'

'For heaven's sake!' Rachel exploded, angry
beyond words.

'In future, when you want to go out—you'll be
escorted. Like it, or not.'

'I don't believe any of this!' She turned towards
the front door, brushing past him, only to be
brought to an abrupt halt as hard hands caught
hold of her arm and swung her round.

'I mean every word of it,' Laz insisted with icy implacability.

'What film-script are you reading from?' she vented furiously. 'One left over from last year's television series?'

'Reality is frequently more electrifying than fiction.'

'Oh *hell*,' Rachel discounted with heavy sarcasm. 'Next, you'll try to convince me I could be in some kind of danger.'

'You want it in words of one syllable?' He looked angry enough to hit her, and at that moment she was so consumed with rage she didn't even care if he did.

'*Please.*'

'All the major newspapers have run photographs of both of us over the past week. After today's press conference, there isn't a newspaper, maga-zine, or television station in the country that won't run articles or footage on my retirement from television. Your face will be seen by millions, linked with mine. You could be accosted by curiosity-seekers and subjected to any number of questions. A few less desirable tabloids might take delight in deliberately setting up a confrontation you would find not only embarrassing, but downright hurtful.' His eyes speared hers, hard and totally merciless. 'Here in celluloid city, publicity is a game with sensationalism as its name. So,' he stressed with dangerous softness. 'We play it by the book, and you have someone along to help deal with any hassling or unpleasant-ness. Simi, if you'd prefer a female companion.'

'Simi?' The thought was abhorrent.

'As well as being adept at fielding queries from persistent fans and reporters,' Laz revealed with wry cynicism. 'She's also a trained expert in martial arts.'

'I'm to be kept a prisoner in a gilded cage,' Rachel voiced with deliberate irony, and he smiled, the edges of his mouth twisting with sardonic humour.

'I want your solemn word that you won't venture out alone.'

'I don't like being given orders.'

His smile deepened. 'I had noticed.'

'Thank heavens it's only for a few weeks,' she declared emotively, unwilling to concede defeat.

'I have your promise there'll be no more bursts of independence?'

For a moment she hesitated, wanting to refuse just for the sheer pleasure of flaunting him, then common-sense surfaced. 'If you insist.'

The pressure on her arm eased, and he trailed gentle fingers down her cheek. 'I do.'

She regarded him with unblinking clarity for an age, becoming caught up in the magical spell he was able to weave without the slightest effort at all. Somehow it only added to the futility of the situation, and she shook her arm free, moving determinedly indoors, feeling too enervated to pursue it any further.

CHAPTER SEVEN

'SIMI will be here in an hour.'

Rachel cradled her coffee mug in both hands, her expression faintly pensive as she took a reviving sip of the hot sweet liquid.

'Shopping,' Laz enlightened with a wry smile. 'Buy whatever you want.'

'I may well do that,' she threatened with grim humour, and encountered his dark musing glance as he stood to his feet.

'I have to leave. Mike is waiting for me in the car.'

'What is it today?' she queried carelessly. 'A practice session?'

'Business first, then I'm due to film both commercials.'

He exuded an inherent vitality, a latent sexuality, that tripped her heartbeat and sent her pulse racing crazily. Attired in slim-fitting cream trousers and a black shirt left unbuttoned at the neck, he presented a potent threat to her peace of mind, and she schooled her composure to remain outwardly calm as she bade coolly.

'Enjoy yourself.'

He crossed round the table and bestowed a teasing, fleeting kiss to the vulnerable curve of her neck. 'You, too.'

A shaft of exquisite pleasure exploded deep within, and she was unable to prevent the faint flaring of her eyes as her senses stirred, tingling into pulsing vibrant life, and she heard his quick

116

indrawn breath an instant before his mouth closed over hers in a kiss that destroyed every defence she'd carefully erected against him.

'I have to go,' Laz declared gently, his eyes dark with a degree of brooding and seeming regret. A hand lifted as he trailed his fingers across her cheek. 'Take care, hmm?' Then straightening, he moved from the kitchen with an easy lithe stride.

Rachel sat at the table in silence for endless long minutes, unable and unwilling to examine the complexity of her emotions, and it was only when Hannah entered the room to begin clearing their breakfast dishes that she quickly rose to her feet.

'I think I'll explore the house.' Her smile was warm and friendly, and she even managed a light laugh. 'I haven't really had the opportunity until now.'

'Would you like me to come with you?' the housekeeper queried pleasantly, and Rachel shook her head.

'No—really, I'll be fine on my own.'

'If there's anything you'd like changed— furniture moved, you have only to say.'

The thought momentarily startled her, and she responded with genuine sincerity—'I can't imagine the necessity.'

As she moved from room to room she could only applaud Laz's choice of interior decor, from the deep-piled cream tufted carpet in every room, the restful mixture of pale blues and greens utilised in curtains and picked out with floral-covered cushioned sofas in the magnificent sun-room with its high bay-windows. The lounge was huge, the colour scheme cream on cream, with deep-seated cream leather sofas and chairs, a splendid chinese rug in blue and cream displayed in the centre of the room, and complemented with matching blue scatter-cushions.

Large and rambling, the downstairs area comprised an elegant entrance foyer tiled in cream marble, to the right of which was the lounge, formal dining-room, and kitchen. The sun-room lay immediately behind the curved staircase, and to the left were situated a sitting-room with television, stereo equipment, video recorder, and a study-cum-library. In a separate wing, adjacent to the garages, were a sound-proofed recording studio and a well-equipped gymnasium and sauna.

The upstairs rooms comprised no less than four bedrooms, each with *en suite* facilities, as well as the master bedroom.

A swimming pool lay in the rear of the grounds, together with a spa-pool and changing-rooms.

All told, it combined into an impressive, but comfortable home that bore expensive but simple elegance, and the antithesis of a symbolic showplace.

Rachel cast her watch a quick glance, then hurried into her bedroom to change, choosing a casually-elegant dress in deep aquamarine, its soft folds accentuating her slim curves.

The thought of spending a few hours, let alone the entire day, in Simi's company was enough to cause Rachel to have serious misgivings.

The fact that she and Simi had never liked each other didn't auger well, and their mutual wariness was apparent as Laz's secretary eased the Mercedes into a parking space some thirty minutes later.

'Have you anything specific in mind?'

Rachel shook her head. 'I know what suits me.' Which was true, for she possessed a flair with colour and design. Her existing wardrobe lacked the sort of elite apparel considered essential among Laz's contemporaries, and she was not averse to the pleasure of spending a considerable amount of money. 'We'll browse until I see something that takes my eye, then take it from there.' She effected a slight shrug. 'Once I've bought clothes, we can start matching them up with shoes and accessories.'

She was determined not to be intimidated in any way, despite Simi's aura of supreme efficiency, and two hours later she'd purchased no less than three dresses, two ensembles suitable for evening wear, and was tentatively mulling the acquisition of a long gown with matching lurex-threaded jacket. In a deeper shade of blue than she normally wore it was daringly cut, and infinitely more sophisticated a design that she'd normally contemplate wearing.

'I need to think about that one,' Rachel decided ruefully, smiling at the saleswoman as she handed her the gown. 'Perhaps we'll come back after lunch, and I'll try it on again.'

'Of course, Mrs Delany. I'll put it aside for you, shall I?'

The name momentarily startled her. She hadn't been called Mrs Delany for years, and she mused wryly that being married to someone with a claim to fame had its compensations, even if she shied from the recognition it brought.

Murmuring her thanks, she walked from the boutique and turned towards Simi to suggest they sit down for ten minutes over coffee.

'There's a nice place just down the road,' Simi concurred, pointing out the striped canopy over the entrance. 'You go in and order while I take these packages back to the car. An espresso for me, nothing to eat.'

The place was well-patronised, and after being shown to a table Rachel ordered a capuccino and an espresso, then mentally recaptured the style and design of the gown while she waited for Simi to appear.

In Los Angeles' favour were the number of excellent boutiques and shops, she mused idly, particularly in vicinity of the exclusive suburbs where millionaire residences were the norm.

'Ah, there you are,' Simi greeted, slipping into the seat opposite. 'Thanks,' she murmured, indicating the coffee. 'I need this.'

The slight inference was there, and Rachel proffered a polite smile. 'I hope you don't find accompanying me too much of a chore.'

Simi didn't return the smile. 'It's what I'm paid to do,' she responded without expression.

'Act as a female bodyguard?' It was a light attempt at humour, and drew a studied riposte.

'I've done it on several occasions in the past.'

'No doubt you have,' Rachel acceded drily, her mind flying to the number of women friends Laz must have entertained over the years. In all probability Simi had been despatched to purchase gifts of jewellery or other similar trinkets as a token for so-called services rendered. More than ten years in his employ as secretary, she would have witnessed many changes—some good, some bad.

'You never approved of Laz's marriage, did you?'

Simi met her gaze without so much as a flicker of emotion. 'His first priority has to be his career. It's very difficult for a wife to understand.'

'Oh, I understood, Simi,' she alluded wryly.

'A wife was a distraction he didn't need—not then.'

'As far as you were concerned—not ever.' Amazing she could sound so calm.

'I've always tried to look after Laz's interests.'

And your own, Rachel added silently. 'So you won't approve of him not taking up the option to renew his television contract?'

'I'm only his secretary,' the other woman declared smoothly. 'Mike, Brad, or Zeke, are the ones to talk to if you want a professional opinion.'

'Off the record, Simi,' she shrugged. 'Surely as Laz's wife, I have a right to know.'

'The series could run for a few more seasons without having a detrimental effect on its popularity.'

'You've been with Laz for several years—long enough to know that any decision he makes is carefully considered and well thought out.'

Simi's eyes narrowed, and her lips thinned into an uncompromising line. 'Do you know he was offered a film contract by one of the major studios? Big budget, top director, and the female lead last year's Oscar nominee for best supporting actress. When he refused, the studio offered him a percentage of the gross as an enticement.' Her eyes glittered with thinly-veiled animosity. 'He had them to a point when he could almost have named his price.'

Rachel considered the remains of her coffee with seeming deliberation, then offered steadily, 'Perhaps he doesn't want to be in movies.'

'Oh, for heaven's sake!' Simi declared emotively. 'People come to Los Angeles in droves to try for that elusive chance, prepared to hack cabs, wait tables—you name it, they'll do it as long as it gives them money with which to hold on that much longer. It's part of the American dream.'

'Laz is already famous in his own right,' Rachel ventured evenly.

'*Yes*, but he could become a legend, command million-dollar fees, if he were to remain in the States.'

She looked up and met Simi's hard staring gaze with equanimity. 'Have you considered that maybe Laz has different values? Money—once it's bought you everything you want and provides an income, becomes superfluous to a degree.' She attempted a smile. 'After all, how many houses can you live in? Or cars can you drive? I'd be a fool if I wasn't aware Laz's royalties from his recordings put him well over the million dollar bracket per year, after taxes and expenses.' Her gaze was remarkably clear. 'Writing music has always been his first love, and you know as well as I do that he's not leaving the States permanently. In all probability he'll commute between Australia and Los Angeles. Maybe, eventually, he'll decide to spend time elsewhere.' She attempted a light shrug. 'Who can say?'

Simi's gaze became slightly vindictive as she sat back and extracted cigarettes and a lighter, her movements jerky as she placed the slim tube between her lips and lit it.

'You've seen what it's like here. The crowds, the fans. They want him on television; out there on stage, performing. He's become what they made him, and he owes it to them to continue—at least for a few more years.' A thin stream of smoke rose in the air, drifting between them before dispersing. 'What if after a few months in Australia, he decides to change his mind?' She paused, then thrust her barb home. 'You couldn't stand the pressures five years ago. Now, they're a hundred times worse. What will you do? Run away again?'

This was it, the moment of truth, Rachel decided. Five years ago Simi was the superior in almost every way. Now, things were not nearly so clear-cut. Aloud, she ventured an answer with sweet civility.

'I'm five years older, Simi—five years wiser. In my inexperience, I imagined Laz found a wife an impossible encumbrance, and detrimental to his career. Something,' she paused deliberately, 'you never hesitated to point out at all too frequent intervals. Oh,' she added with a measure of cynicism, 'I don't hold it against you. Not now. Laz couldn't have wished for a more loyal employee. Except, somewhere along the way, your ideals for him took a different turn from those he had for himself.' She was really on her mettle now, *sure*, and undeniably in command. 'Why deny Laz his share of personal happiness?' she queried equably. 'Something he considers holds more importance in his life than a greater degree of success than he now has; or wealth, for that matter. He wants time with his wife—*me*—the hope of children.' Her voice strengthened with steadfast certainty. 'I left Laz alone to pursue his career in any direction he chose to take it. The decision is *his*, Simi, not mine. Accept it.'

The older woman drained the last of her coffee, then said evenly, 'Shall we go?'

Without a word Rachel rose to her feet and preceded Simi from the bistro.

As they reached the pavement she turned back towards the boutique they'd patronised earlier.

'Are you sure?' Simi queried. 'That gown is not really you.'

As an attempt to undermine her confidence, it didn't succeed. Five years was a long time, and she was no longer an insecure young bride in awe of all things Hollywood—including every member of her husband's entourage.

'Yes. What's more, I'm going to have those scarlet silk evening trousers with matching top and jacket.'

Simi's only response was a brief considering look that was more eloquent than any words she might have uttered.

After that came shoes, and Rachel bought several pairs, loving the elegant evening sandals with their fine rolled-leather straps, one pair in gold, another in silver.

'Lunch,' she decided at one o'clock. 'Let's despatch these into the boot of the car, then find somewhere to eat.' Just to prove her independence, she named one of the most expensive restaurants in town, one well-known for its famous clientele.

'I'm not sure Laz would approve.'

Perhaps not, but Rachel was beyond caring. 'Nonsense,' she determined blandly. 'He gave me distinct instructions to enjoy myself.'

'We don't have a reservation,' Simi reminded with slight impatience, and Rachel directed a stunning smile.

'Then you must 'phone for one.' Part of her deplored the way she was acting, but some inner gremlin was pushing for her to prove superiority, and this seemed one way of doing it! 'I'm sure the mention of Laz's name will carry sufficient weight—plus the promise of a suitable gratuitous tip. You must know the number. You can use the 'phone in the car.'

Afterwards Rachel wasn't so sure it had been a good idea. In fact, she couldn't imagine what on earth possessed her to insist on frequenting such hallowed ground. Without exception, every woman present was groomed to the nth degree, looking as if they'd spent the entire morning with their hairdresser, beautician, manicurist, preparing themselves to appear for lunch. The men, on the other hand, bore a casual elegance that appeared deliberately contrived.

Champagne, in fact anything even mildly alcoholic, was definitely out. For however long it took to indulge in a seemingly leisurely meal, a clear head was definitely a must!

'Perrier,' she ordered, and when the waiter appeared she chose a small salad, following it with a compote of fresh fruit.

At the prices the restaurant charged it was obvious its patrons came to be seen, rather than merely to eat, Rachel perceived somewhat wryly as she glimpsed the amount on the bill Simi signed almost an hour later. It was more than she and Millie paid for a month's groceries.

Just as they were leaving the restaurant she became aware of a few covert glances from a group of women standing near the entrance, and she saw one nudge another and heard penetrating snatches of conversation.

'It's her, I tell you. I saw her on television last night.'

'Are you sure?'

'Of course I'm sure. She was with Laz, so it has to be.'

'Well, go on. Ask her.'

'Where the *hell* is the boy with the car,' Simi muttered beneath her breath as one of the women, obviously elected spokeswoman, descended on them.

'You're Laz Delany's wife, aren't you?'

'Don't say a word,' Simi hissed, and Rachel gave a faint smile.

'Is it really true Laz is giving up his television series?'

'All relevant information was given to the press,' Simi intervened with smooth professionalism, catching hold of Rachel's arm, urging her away.

'What sort of woman are you to make him give up his career?'

'Can't you live in the States?' The woman persisted, this time with a degree of truculence. 'Why Australia?'

'Get into the car,' Simi bade as the Mercedes slid to a halt. 'Lock the door.'

Rachel didn't hesitate, and Simi slipped in behind the wheel to send the vehicle surging forward with superb competence.

'Where to, now?'

The scene had been so brief, almost farcical, that Rachel felt more inclined to believe she'd dreamt the whole thing. 'Beverly Hills,' she instructed aloud, and incurred Simi's bleak stare.

Consequently it was well after five when they arrived home, and Rachel murmured her thanks as Simi relinquished the Mercedes into Hank's care.

Indoors, she made straight for the stairs and her bedroom, praying that Laz wasn't already in, or that Simi wouldn't report the altercation that had taken place outside the restaurant.

Stripping down to her bra and pants, she crossed to the wardrobe and selected a pale blue tracksuit and donned it, then tidied her hair before emerging out on to the landing to meet Hank coming halfway up the stairs.

'I'll put these in one of the spare rooms,' he

intimated, his arms full of various sized packages. 'Hannah will unpack them for you later.'

'There's no hurry,' she assured with a smile. 'Tomorrow will do fine.'

Downstairs she moved into the kitchen, ascertained what time dinner was due to be served, then made for the sitting-room on the opposite side of the house with the intention of writing a letter to her mother.

Twenty minutes later she'd managed to fill a few pages of tritely-written paragraphs full of apparent enthusiasm in descriptive phrases covering events of the past week. A faint grimace twisted her lips as she skimmed the neat handwriting. No one reading it would guess she was filled with self-doubt, her emotions so contrary they continually swung like a pendulum between pride and passion, or that her nerves waged war as she battled to project a serene façade with Laz's numerous associates and friends.

At night, in bed and alone together, she could temporarily forget for the space of a few hours that the man holding her close was Laz Delany, television superstar and recording megastar. Then there was no doubt in her mind their love could surmount every known obstacle. It was only with the dawn that all her insecurities emerged afresh to taunt her, compounding the knowledge that Laz needed a special kind of love—one that was able to allow room for his career, a freedom to give rein to his creative talent and all that it involved without manipulative matrimonial strings.

Maybe—just maybe, she could. When the fighting stopped, and the anger she harboured against him had the opportunity to subside. Now, she needed time to come to terms with priorities—

her own, as well as his. And a sense of humour to cope with the next few weeks!

'There you are.'

Rachel glanced up, her reverie broken by the sound of that deep drawling voice, and she summoned a quick smile as she neatly folded the pages and slid them into an envelope.

'As you can see—writing a letter home.'

Laz moved across the room with lithe easy strides, his expression enigmatic in the early evening light. 'Feel free to 'phone whenever you want,' he indicated with a faint shrug, and his mouth curved with wry humour. 'I can afford the calls.'

'Thanks,' she acknowledged evenly. 'I'd prefer to write.'

'Another attempt to oppose me, Rachel?'

Something in his voice caused a quiver of alarm, and she determinedly held his penetrating gaze. For a moment she considered pretending ignorance, but such a course would not only insult his intelligence, but her own. Aloud, she parried evenly—'You've spoken to Simi?'

'Indeed,' he drawled with hateful cynicism. 'Perhaps you'll enlighten me as to just what you're trying to prove?'

Now, there was a good question! If she knew, she could easily answer. 'Doubtless your inestimable secretary was empowered to report verbatim my every word and movement,' she declared with unaccustomed flippancy. 'I also spent up largely. Your charge accounts will be quite enormous.'

'I distinctly recollect telling you to buy anything you wanted,' Laz declared drily, and she retaliated swiftly.

'Believe me, I did!'

'I don't give a damn about how much you spent,' he inferred with dangerous softness. 'That's not what we're talking about, and you know it.'

'Oh, I'm sorry,' she apologised, her eyes wide with deliberate guile. 'I lunched with the elite, and shouldn't have.'

'You know damn well why.'

She drew a deep breath and expelled it slowly. 'I didn't expect to be recognised. If I had, I would have donned a wig and gloried in anonymity!' A sudden gleam of wry amusement lit her eyes, making them appear a clear sparkling blue. 'Remember the false moustache you affixed one night we dined out?' A tiny bubble of laughter emerged from her throat. 'I was terrified it would come loose and fall into your soup!'

'Don't evade the issue.'

'Where's your sense of humour?'

He didn't immediately answer, and his eyes darkened measurably. 'I lost it,' he alluded with quiet cynicism. 'Around the time Lennon was killed.'

She was silent for several long seconds, her expression sobering and becoming serious. 'You've made your point,' she said quietly, and his lips twisted to form a wry grimace.

'Just remember it.'

The need to say something—anything, prompted her to rush heedlessly into speech. 'When do you start cutting your new album?'

'The boys and I get together on Monday to run it through.' His voice was deliberately bland, his expression enigmatic. 'If everything goes well, we should be able to cut the first track towards the end of the week.'

'And the commercials?' She endeavoured to

keep her tone light. 'Weren't you taping them today? Did you get them both finished?'

'One,' Laz informed drily. 'Unfortunately the female model was unaware of an allergy condition, and it wasn't until we'd started the umpteenth take that someone had the presence of mind to suggest her sneezing attacks might be due to more than the cool afternoon breeze.'

'Sure it wasn't the cologne you were promoting?'

'Possibly,' he drawled. 'The agency is sending along a replacement model tomorrow.'

He was standing too close, his proximity unfurling a multitude of sensations deep within, and a tell-tale pulse at the base of her throat began to quicken in recognition of his intrinsic brand of sexual magnetism.

She wanted to rise to her feet and move away from him, mention dinner, the weather—*anything*. Mesmerised fascination kept her motionless, the pupils of her eyes dilating as he lifted a hand and caught hold of her chin.

'I've had a hard day,' he inclined with a deep husky murmur. 'Would it be asking too much to expect a wifely kiss?'

Rachel swallowed convulsively, the tip of her tongue edging out in a purely nervous gesture as it traced along her lower lip, and she saw his eyes flare briefly, then his hands closed over her shoulders, lifting her towards him.

His mouth was warm and infinitely passionate as it fastened on hers, and of their own volition her arms crept up to wind themselves round his neck.

The slow warmth that had begun deep in the pit of her stomach spread until her whole body seemed caught up with tremulous aching sensation, and she gave a tiny exultant gasp as his hands slid down her back, urging her closer against his lean hard length so that she could be in no doubt of his arousal.

Not content, one hand slid beneath the jacket of her tracksuit, curving down over her gently-rounded bottom, while the other slipped over her ribcage to capture her breast.

'Laz.' It was a token protest at best, and his eyes were alive with teasing warmth as he mocked gently——

'Laz—*what*?' A slow smile curved his generous sensually-moulded mouth.

'We should both change ready for dinner.'

His silent laugh did strange things to her equilibrium, and she gave a faint gasp as his lips brushed against her temple.

'If that means we get to go upstairs to the bedroom, then I can't help but agree,' he intimated with evocative deliberation, letting his tongue trail gently over the delicate ridges of her ear.

'I'm not sure that's such a good idea.'

'Hmm, why not?'

He was teasing her, taking delight in the soft pink colour that slowly crept over her cheeks. 'You know very well why not,' she responded a trifle fiercely, and he chuckled deep in his throat.

'Dinner won't be ready until eight. That gives us an hour.' His lips slid down the sensitive pulsing cord at the edge of her neck to settle in a vulnerable hollow, teasing, tantalising in a manner that made the blood course through her veins like liquid fire. 'Come share my shower, then love me, let me pleasure and love you.' His mouth moved up and hovered gently above her own. 'I need the sweet heaven I find in your arms.'

A faint tremor shook her slim frame, and she linked her hands together, holding his head down to hers. 'An hour?' she teased, her eyes alive with sparkling warmth, and he gave a soft laugh.

'I'm sure Hannah will understand if we're late.'

Rachel closed her eyes and buried her head against his neck as he placed an arm beneath her knees and carried her from the room, too caught up with the mystical magic he promised to care whether they ate or not, or at what hour. There was only *now*, and their mutual need of each other.

CHAPTER EIGHT

SATURDAY evening's concert was an incredible success. Every seat in the huge auditorium was filled, and from her position back-stage Rachel could only admire Laz's faultless fluidity as he moved from one song to another.

His rapport with the audience was magical, and they seemed loath to let him leave, demanding and receiving an encore before Laz moved off stage and Mike hustled them both out a side door and into the waiting car.

Rachel had dressed with care, electing to wear one of her new gowns, the deep blue ensemble with matching jacket, and she sat in silence as the limousine transported them to the restaurant where the party was being held.

Laz seemed quiet, almost preoccupied, and when she commended his performance he simply inclined his head, then caught hold of her hand and lifted it to his lips, gently kissing each finger in turn.

'Don't be nervous,' he murmured softly.

He was too perceptive by far! 'It's impossible for anyone to like me,' she ventured quietly. 'Women envy what I have—*you*; and any men associated with your career resent me.'

The room was crowded, and alive with seemingly innumerable guests bent on enjoying themselves. Champagne flowed like water, and the food was superb.

When Mike materialised out of the crowd and

drew Laz into an earnest discussion, Rachel let her gaze wander idly round the room, admiring the flawless beauty of many of the women present.

'So you're Laz Delany's wife.'

Rachel turned slightly towards the large bearded man standing at her side. 'I have that—dubious honour,' she acknowledged with equanimity.

'Ah—you possess a sense of humour,' he accorded drolly, and a faint twinkle lit the depths of her eyes.

'Not all of the time.'

'A realist—I like that.'

'And a little out of place in fantasy-land,' she ventured wryly, and he gave a soft laugh.

'Honest, too.'

'So many famous faces,' Rachel mused, glancing round the large room. 'I feel as if I'm treading on glass. Everyone here is *somebody*.'

'And you're not suitably awed?'

She looked at him in silence for several seconds, then said quietly, 'Should I be?'

'Refreshing,' he declared drily. 'The usual response is an ecstatic averral.'

'Accompanied by a desire to aspire to fame?'

'And you don't?'

Her gaze was remarkably level. 'Laz alone has more fame than I can cope with.'

'I imagine he handles it well enough for both of you.'

That was nothing less than the truth. Laz had few pretentions about himself, or his work. If she wanted to fault him, it would be with the wary cynicism he'd acquired. Doubtlessly an essential requisite to survive in the world of showbusiness.

'Will you hold it against me if I ask what it is that you do?'

His deep hearty chuckle brought a faint smile, and she effected a wry grimace.

'Oh dear,' she sighed ruefully. 'I've undoubtedly damaged your ego by failing to recognise who you are.'

'As you're not an American, I'll find it in my heart to forgive you.'

'Perhaps you'd better tell me before I step even deeper into the mire.'

'I'm one of your class movie directors,' he imparted with sardonic humour.

'Well-known, obviously,' Rachel declared solemnly, and he inclined his head in silent acknowledgement.

'There are some who think so.'

'Do you enjoy directing?'

'That's a rare question. I'm usually asked what it's like to work with superstars.' He lifted a hand and fingered his beard, his hard dark eyes softening somewhat as he gazed at her in thoughtful contemplation. 'Occasionally I do. When the script shows an elusive illusory quality that promises magic—if only it can be portrayed precisely that way on screen. I regard the transition as my own personal challenge. It's a question of everything being *right*—contracting the actors and actresses you instinctively know are the only choice for each respective part, having them all be in accord with what should be achieved, rather than wanting to express their individual interpretation, hiring the best technicians and crew, *feeling* the gradual increase of excitement as everyone on the set begins to sense this particular movie might be more than just *good*. That it eventually *is*, and receives critical acclaim——' His faint smile was strangely sad.

'Ah, one constantly struggles, striving for that elusive mystical perfection. Occasionally it happens, and I have the satisfaction of knowing, as does everyone else in the industry, that there is nothing else to touch it.'

Rachel gave a sudden start as she felt a touch on her arm, and she glanced round to see Laz had moved back to her side.

'You both seem to be in the midst of a very earnest conversation,' Laz declared with an indolent smile, and the other man gave an eloquent shrug.

'We merely pursued an interesting topic with which to fill the time.' His glance moved from Laz to Rachel. 'And now, if you will excuse me?'

'Darling!' a soft feminine voice intruded, the slightly husky tones infinitely sensual and hinting reproach. 'You were marvellous tonight, absolutely incredible.'

Rachel felt an unenviable measure of jealousy rise to the surface, and because of it, her smile became even more radiant than before, adding to the terrible strain involved in presenting an affable façade.

Laz turned slightly and inclined his head in polite, smiling acknowledgement. 'Thank you. Rachel—a friend of mine, Annabel Simmons.'

She was gorgeous—utterly, and without visible fault, Rachel perceived on seeing the tall willowy auburn-haired beauty stunningly attired in figure-hugging black, the bodice of which dipped alarmingly low front and back, with a hem split to above mid-thigh. Her only jewellery was a huge square-cut topaz ring worn on her left hand and given emphasis by long bronze-tipped nails.

Friend? Rachel queried silently. Annabel

Simmons was no man's *friend*. Any more than was Melissa Kiernan. *God*. By comparison, she felt like a nobody, sharing nothing in common with any of these beautiful plastic people all equally intent on outdoing each other.

'So—you're off to Australia,' Annabel breathed with overt deliberation, somehow managing by subtle emphasis to make his destination sound like the uncouth wilds on the opposite side of the world. 'To play the gentleman farmer, I believe.' Her soft laugh tinkled with attractive distinction, seemingly uncontrived, and she lifted a hand to touch his arm, her expression vaguely hungry as her manicured fingers appreciated the taut muscular strength beneath their tips. 'One can only hope such an inclination is but a mere passing fancy. Anything else would be such a terrible waste.'

Laz appeared amused, damn him! 'You think so?' he drawled. 'I hope it's going to be very productive.'

'What a loaded statement, darling.' She ran her fingers along his forearm, and pouted when he removed them. 'Somehow I can't see you raising chickens and growing avocados.'

'A very competent manager takes care of that for me,' he acceded cynically. All I have in mind is writing music, and loving my wife.' The last was offered gently, almost as a reminder, and he added with damnable amusement, 'Although not necessarily in that order.'

Rachel almost choked, and endeavoured to hide her embarrassment as he leaned forward to brush his lips against her temple.

'I have to admire you, Rachel,' Annabel accorded with saccharine sweetness. 'Whatever it is you possess, it must be incredibly potent.' Her glance swept from head to foot with encompassing swift assessment before swinging back to Laz. 'Hidden fires, darling?' A contrived moue became a sulky pout. 'What is it that Rachel has, and all of us lack?'

'Ah,' he murmured sardonically, his eyes darkly amused. 'I'm not about to tell you.'

'But you must,' Annabel protested. 'However else am I to understand where I've failed?'

Laz's expression assumed wry cynicism. 'I was never a prize to be won,' he alluded drily.

Rachel wanted to extricate herself from the arm draped about her waist, and move away. Except there was nowhere she could go that mightn't place her in a more potentially explosive situation. At least anchored to Laz's side she was relatively safe. Or was she?

No sooner had Annabel detached herself for other pastures than Melissa Kiernan glided forward to take her place!

'Laz!' A carefully-effected grimace twisted her glossy lips. 'One almost has to stand in line to gain a moment of your time.'

'That bad, hmm?' he concurred wryly, giving her a slow warm smile. 'How are you?'

Was it Rachel's imagination, or did she detect a hidden meaning behind that seemingly careless query? It was getting to be a diabolical habit of late, reading any number of reasons behind every phrase Laz uttered. Not only was it harrowing on her nerves, it played havoc with her senses.

'Surviving.' Melissa turned towards Rachel, and her smile seemed to be genuine as she proclaimed lightly, 'This can't be easy for you.'

'I can't begin to compete,' she responded evenly,

tentatively expecting a stinging reply, and was vaguely surprised when none was forthcoming.

'On the contrary, there's no one in this room to touch you.'

Rachel felt her eyes widen, and a hint of amusement lit their depths. 'A compliment?'

'Definitely.'

'Perhaps you'd better stay and talk a while,' Laz mused humorously, silent laughter crinkling the corners of his eyes. 'Rachel was beginning to feel desperate.'

'Thanks,' she accorded wrily, and the actress gave a faint grimace.

'Try and make believe we're friends—which I think we can be.' A definite sparkle lit her eyes. 'At least we'll give the gossips reason for conjecture.' Faint bitterness edged her voice. 'Reconciled wife and supposed ex-lover together, talking. They'll hold their breath waiting for the sparks to fly.'

Rachel was speechless for a few seconds, then she managed with remarkable aplomb, 'Perhaps with good reason. Your names have been coupled together on several occasions.' Lord, she sounded calm. Inside she was hurting so much it was a wonder the pain wasn't visible to everyone in the room.

Melissa's eyes seemed to mirror regret, and something else—compassion? It was hardly possible.

'Publicity,' the actress accorded quietly. 'Directed by the studio heads to engender maximum interest in their coveted series. While you're striving to climb aboard that first step on the ladder to success you actively seek the photographers' eye. If by chance, and talent, you make it anywhere near the top, you become much more selective, only deigning to give a few selected interviews. Ironic, isn't it?'

Rachel inclined her head in silent agreement, her gaze unconsciously wandering the room.

Among these people she felt like a fish out of water, unwilling to put out the feelers of friendship for fear of being eaten alive.

'Laz—darling.'

Rachel recognised the woman immediately as being an actress who'd made guest appearances on several popular television series, and who, if gossip could be believed, was in the running to head a series of her own. Perfection personified, her slender figure outlined beneath a stunning gown, ash-blonde hair that cascaded to her shoulders, and styled into a carelessly-contrived mane, tasteful make-up that wasn't in the least extravagant, merely utilised to heighten her finely-moulded features.

'You don't mind if I join you?'

'Jackie,' Laz acknowledged, attending to the necessary introductions with urbane sophistication before offering—'I believe you're set to shoot the first episode early next month.' Smiling, he lifted his glass. 'Here's to success.'

'Thanks, darling. Pray like mad for me, won't you?' A sultry laugh emerged from her lips as she looked at him, her eyes almost eating him alive. 'Naughty of you to escape. I rather wanted you to support me by guesting on my show. Sure I can't do anything to change your mind?'

His expression assumed amused regret. 'Not a chance.'

'Hmn,' Jackie murmured, subjecting Rachel to a raking head-to-toe appraisal that made her burn with embarrassed indignation. 'You're not American, are you?'

'Will you hold it against me?' Rachel queried civilly, taking the sting out of the words by proffering a smile.

'Australian.' Somehow she made it sound like a remote unknown continent hardly worth the mention. 'I remember reading it somewhere.' Elegant silver-tipped fingers trailed with deliberate provocation over the slim gold chain at the base of her throat, her eyes hungrily fixed on Laz. 'You must give me your address.'

Laz regarded her with indolent amusement. 'So you can visit?'

'But of course, darling. We go back a long way.' The pouting moue was just right, and Rachel endeavoured to stifle the uncharitable thought that the actress must have practised it constantly to achieve the desired effect.

'Anyone wanting to contact me will have to go through Mike, I'm afraid.'

Even Rachel recognised it as a subtle brush-off, and she watched with idle fascination as Jackie summoned a brilliant smile.

'One can only hope you know what you're doing, Laz. In this industry one needs to be seen to be constantly working, otherwise you're dead.' Her gaze swept towards Rachel and back again. 'One—two years from now, I trust you'll still think she's worth it.'

'Cat,' Melissa accorded beneath her breath the instant the blonde actress was out of hearing, then muttered an unladylike curse. 'Oh-oh, here comes another.'

It was too much for Rachel, and proffering a fixed smile she indicated a need to visit the powder-room, moving away before Laz had the opportunity to stop her.

Once there, she took as long as she dared ensuring her hair, her make-up, were beyond criticism, then summoning a reserve of courage she turned towards the door and narrowly missed having it swing against her as someone else entered the room.

Attired in startling white, the woman's black hair contrasted sharply with her smooth cream skin, and even as Rachel made to sidestep past her the woman turned, her exquisite features becoming sharp with recognition.

'You're Laz Delany's wife. I saw you on television.'

She could hardly deny it, and she gave a slight smile in silent acknowledgement.

'Please don't go. I'd love to talk to you.'

This could only lead from bad to worse, and Rachel wanted no part of it. 'Excuse me, I really have to go back.'

The other woman moved quickly, effectively blocking the door, and Rachel felt sickened by the avid speculation evident.

'A few minutes, that's all.'

'For what?' she queried steadily. 'An off-the-record in-depth interview on what it's like to be Laz Delany's wife?' Her gaze remained steady. 'If you are a reporter you must think me incredibly naïve to imagine I'd answer those sort of questions. Now, please let me pass.'

The woman didn't move, and Rachel adopted a firm approach.

'You realise that in detaining me, I could lay a complaint against you for harrassment?'

'It would be my word against yours.'

Rachel drew a deep calming breath. 'Perhaps you should be reminded that my husband is not without influence. If you value your job, I'd strongly advise you to let me leave—now.'

'Doesn't it bother you that Laz has been unfaithful on countless occasions?' The brunette's eyes glittered like topaz. 'I've followed every aspect of his career for years, and I have some very impressive data.'

I just bet you have, Rachel determined ruefully, wondering precisely what was behind the woman's motive. She daren't resort to a display of temper, yet the temptation was almost impossible to resist. 'For the last time—will you please step out of my way?'

'He's fantastic in bed, isn't he?' The accompanying laugh was slightly off-key. 'Every woman's dream of the ideal lover.'

There was no way she was going to verify or deny it—which was precisely what the other woman was trying to goad her to do. *Keep calm*, she bade silently. It was only a matter of time before she would be able to escape this ugly scene. Sooner or later someone was bound to enter the powder-room.

'Even at twenty, he possessed a devastating sex appeal. God, to think I let him slip through my fingers!'

There was little doubt the woman had worked herself into a highly traumatic state, and she seemed to be teetering on the brink of mental instability. Perhaps it might be wiser just to stand still and appear to listen, Rachel decided warily.

'That he should choose *you*—a nobody from nowhere! You're not even exceptionally beautiful.'

At that moment the door swung inwards, and Rachel didn't hesitate as she moved swiftly past two faintly startled women straight into the path of Melissa.

'I've been despatched on a mercy mission. Laz was getting concerned.'

As well he should be! 'I needed a respite from all his adulating—friends,' she alluded wryly, and Melissa gave a slight grimace.

'Be grateful it's almost over.'

That was highly doubtful. Women would still fawn all over Laz when he reached sixty—even seventy! A hollow laugh died in her throat. If she was going to stay the distance, she'd need to cultivate more than a sense of humour!

Laz's faintly narrowed glance swept over her in a swift encompassing appraisal, and without a word he took hold of her arm. 'Let's go.'

'Likewise,' Melissa declared with droll cynicism. 'I've done my duty to society tonight.'

Rachel didn't utter a word as they began threading their way towards the door, and once in the lobby while waiting for their respective cars to be brought round she barely registered the dinner invitation Melissa proffered for the following evening, finding it a tremendous relief to slip into the rear seat of the chauffeured limousine ahead of Laz, then be transported swiftly, competently, home.

'Okay, let's have it.'

They were barely indoors, and Rachel turned towards the stairs with the intention of going straight up to bed. The last thing she wanted was a post-mortem on *any* part of the evening—much less what had transpired in the powder-room.

'Didn't I shine with sufficient radiance?' Heavens, she'd better not start, otherwise she'd never stop! 'Or maybe it was my lack of sparkling wit?' She threw him a withering glance. 'Sorry, Laz. I'm no hypocrite.'

He stood there regarding her in silence, one

hand thrust into his trouser pocket, the other lifting to rake through his hair. 'We had to attend. It was unavoidable.'

'As well as me having to fend off countless snide remarks, I suppose?' A bitter laugh left her throat. 'Perhaps I should call a press conference of my own—something along the lines of "My husband, the sex symbol. A day and a night in the life of Rachel Delany".' Her lips twisted with weary cynicism. 'We mustn't forget the nights. That's what they all want to know about.'

His eyes narrowed and became hooded. 'You know damned well that ninety per cent of gossip is speculative conjecture.'

'Really? You mean I need only concern myself with a paltry *ten* per cent? How abstemious of you!'

'Rachel,' Laz warned emotively. 'If I did a fraction of the things my publicity has me purporting to do, I'd be a physical wreck. No one can attend all-night parties, bed an endless number of women, and still get to the studio at five in the morning six days out of seven and work a twelve to sixteen hour day, *and* learn lines for the following day's filming.'

She was too caught up in a turmoil of anger and humiliation to heed him. 'I should never have let you coerce me into coming back here in the first place. I should have stopped it before it began by 'phoning my mother from the house in Brisbane and telling her you'd ridden roughshod over me, and that your inclination for us to get back together was not necessarily *mine*!'

'Go upstairs to bed, before I'm tempted to do something I might later regret,' he bit out hardily, and she rounded on him in fury.

'Don't you dare play the heavy husband. I *am* going to bed—but not *yours*.'

'The hell you're not.' His voice was silky smooth and dangerous.

Suddenly he was close, much too close, and she turned to flee the stairs, only to trip halfway up and fall into an ignominious heap on her hands and knees. Even as she scrambled to her feet hard hands caught and lifted her high.

'Put me down!'

'Eventually.'

'You damned egotistical bastard!' Rachel vented, so furious she was almost crying in her rage.

He hefted her effortlessly all the way to their bedroom, then hardly shifting his hold he let her slide down to her feet.

The instant her hands were free she lashed out at him, hearing the explosive crack as her hand connected with his face, and she gazed in horror as the red mark on his cheek darkened and became clearly visible.

For a wild moment she thought he meant to strike her back, and she actually flinched in anticipation, only to cry out in startled surprise as he hauled her across his knee to render a bruisingly painful spanking.

Then, almost without pause, he drew her down on to the bed and forcibly held her immobile before lowering his mouth over hers in a kiss that was nothing less than brutally savage.

It was useless attempting to struggle, and after a few futile minutes Rachel didn't even try. As a punishment it was decidedly effective, and her mouth, her tongue, *throbbed* as he ravished at will.

Not content, he proceeded to remove her clothes, then his own, and with slow deliberation he brought alive every pulsing nerve-centre, callously searing her tender flesh whenever she berated him, until at last she moaned in capitulation, clinging to him like a begging wanton.

His deep wounding aggression made her gasp out loud, then she became caught up in the steady spiral of sensation that swamped her mind and carried her high on to a plateau of mutual ecstasy so intense she wasn't aware of anything except a bewitching euphoric enchantment.

Afterwards she lay still, doubtful of her body's capability to generate the slightest movement.

'You diabolical fiend.' It was meant to be an accusation, but somehow it came out as a husky emotionless whisper.

'Don't expect an apology. You deserved everything you got.'

'It was all your fault.'

There was silence for a few infinitesimal seconds, then Laz drawled with weary cynicism——

'Isn't it always?'

Rachel was too tired to even cry, and she gave up the struggle against total oblivion as her eyelids drooped slowly closed.

CHAPTER NINE

'TRY and smile,' Laz bade as he eased the Mercedes down the long winding road.

Below lay a panoramic tracery of streetlights, which from this distance seemed little more than pinpricks in the darkness.

Rachel didn't even bother to look at him, and kept her attention fastened on the scene beyond the tinted glass window. 'You can't expect me to view the evening with enthusiasm.'

His glance was swift and analytical. 'An enjoyable meal spent in pleasant company—without the inevitable interruptions of dining in a restaurant. Surely it has advantages?'

'Somehow the thought of Melissa lovingly preparing tempting fare doesn't fill me with joy.' A faintly bitter laugh left her lips. 'She might be planning a Lucrezia Borgia scenario in which I get to be poisoned.'

'There are times when I could beat you senseless,' Laz accorded with dangerous softness, and she bit back a swift retort, proffering instead——

'No doubt you could. But I refuse to vie with another woman for your attention.' A humourless laugh bubbled to the surface. 'That should definitely be plural—there are so many beautiful young things who would almost *die* for so much as a smile from you.'

With a muttered oath he pulled over to the kerb and stopped the car. Switching off the ignition, he turned towards her, placing an elbow on the steering wheel as he leaned forward. 'Melissa is a friend, a very good one,' he began hardily. 'She will have gone to a lot of trouble on our behalf, and I'd be grateful if you'll at least be polite.'

His expression was hard to determine in the dim interior of the car, but it was impossible not to sense his anger.

'I didn't plan on being anything else.'

'Dammit, Rachel,' Laz bit out emotively. 'Isn't it about time you gave me the benefit of the doubt?'

'So, in spite of innumerable photographs showing Melissa clinging very closely to your arm, the undeniable fact you've maintained a—friendship, with her for several years, I'm honestly expected to believe it's nothing more than platonic?'

'I give you my word.'

She wanted desperately to believe him, but the evidence was hardly in his favour. 'Can't we discuss this later?' She didn't want to think about it, much less discuss it. 'We shouldn't keep Melissa waiting.'

He directed her a hard glance, then with a muffled curse he turned on the ignition and sent the car moving swiftly forward.

Rachel had little recollection of where they were heading, or how long it took to reach their destination, and she didn't offer so much as a word as the Mercedes turned down a long dirveway, then slowed to a halt before an illuminated entrance.

Laz slipped from behind the wheel as she slid out and closed her door, and just as they reached the lower step, the front door opened to reveal none other than Melissa herself in its aperture.

Greetings dispensed with, they preceded her indoors and were shown into a large, comfortably-furnished lounge.

Rachel was glad she'd elected to wear the scarlet silk evening trousers with matching top and jacket. With slender high-heeled gold sandals, it lent an air of sophistication and gave a necessary boost to her self-confidence.

She was aware of Laz's hand on her arm, urging her forward, and her eyes widened involuntarily at the sight of a man seated on the far side of the room. It wasn't so much that he was seated, when etiquette demanded otherwise, but that his chair was a wheelchair.

Her eyes were riveted on that kindly face, the deep brown eyes, and his smile was gentle, without a glimmer of self-pity as he used his hands to propel the wheelchair forward.

'Rachel,' he acknowledged warmly. 'I've heard so much about you.'

'My husband, Ben,' Melissa introduced quietly, and Rachel took his outstretched hand, feeling its strength as he clasped her own.

'Laz,' Ben indicated, a genuine smile creasing his features. 'It's good to see you again.'

'And you.'

'The trip was successful.' This was more of a statement than a question, and Laz smiled.

'Yes. I managed to persuade Rachel to return with me.'

That wasn't strictly true, but she let it pass, and when Melissa offered them drinks she requested a martini, feeling definitely in need of something alcoholic.

Dinner was served half an hour later; an elaborate meal consisting of four courses, accompanied by excellent wines and splendid conversation, some of which was highly illuminating.

'Very few people know of my existence,' Ben revealed over coffee, glancing keenly towards Rachel before offering his wife a singularly sweet smile. 'Melissa is very protective of me, and Laz has been a staunch, loyal friend to both of us.'

What could she say? Almost anything at all would sound banal, so she simply smiled.

'Publicity releases portray me as an unattached female,' Melissa informed, giving a short laugh. 'An image I try hard to maintain—with a little help from my friends. Ben and I were childhood sweethearts, marrying while we were both still in college. Then came Vietnam,' she continued with a slight catch in her voice. 'Ben went away walking strong and tall, and came back in a wheelchair. With a few exceptions he's worth ten of any man I know. Six years ago I was an actress struggling for recognition, until Laz pushed me to audition for a part in his television series. It's thanks to him I'm where I am today.' She paused, then continued deliberately—'Earning a hundred times more than I ever could as a shop assistant. It has meant I've been able to have this home specially designed to suit Ben's individual needs, pay for live-in help, and buy every conceivable device to make his life as comfortable as humanly possible.' Lifting her cup to her lips she took a generous sip before replacing it on to the saucer. 'The publicity department came up with the idea that as Laz and I were romantically linked together in the series, it would look good if we were seen and photographed together around town. Ben was happy, because not only was Laz an ideal escort, he was also someone he knew and trusted—despite what the gossip columnists wrote to the contrary. By the time the series was in its third season, I had gained sufficient recognition to warrant film offers—good ones. Now I have a multi-million dollar contract with an option for renewal. Ben and I will be set for life,' she concluded softly.

Somehow Rachel managed to get through what remained of the evening—smiling, talking, even laughing on occasion. Yet beneath the surface she experienced a mixture of angry regret that Laz had chosen this method of attempting to prove his innocence—with Melissa, at least.

'You deliberately set it up, didn't you?' she demanded within minutes of them leaving the house, and Laz waited to reply until he'd cleared the driveway.

'The power of the press is damning—and damnable,' he declared, urging the car forward. 'There appeared little alternative but to provide you with positive proof.'

Rachel kept her eyes directly on the scene beyond the windscreen, and her voice held a measure of sarcasm. 'Do you intend dispensing with each and every one of your so-called women friends in a similar manner?' She paused slightly, then continued—'How many other evenings of enlightenment am I to be subjected to?'

'Would you believe—none?'

'I see,' she acknowledged in a tight little voice.

'Do you, Rachel?' he drawled imperturbably, and she nodded briefly.

'Oh, yes. With the number of women chasing after you, it would be impossible to imagine none of them caught you.'

'Ah, whatever happened to trust?'

At the wry edge of humour in his voice she

rounded on him with ill-concealed fury. 'We've been apart for five years. I'd have to be incredibly naïve to believe in your fidelity!'

'Jealous, Rachel?'

Even the thought of that strong lithe body making love to another woman—*women*, made her feel positively ill. 'No, of course not,' she threw stiltedly.

'The ultimate in all the virtues—a realistic, understanding wife,' he mocked hatefully, and it was all she could do not to turn on him and deliver a furious tirade.

She sat in rigid silence for the remaining ten minutes it took to reach their secluded hillside mansion, and the instant the car drew to a halt inside the garage she slipped out and waited tight-lipped for him to unlock the front door.

As soon as they were indoors she made straight for the stairs, only to come to an abrupt halt as hands closed over her arms, tightening with painful intensity as she began to struggle.

'I want to go to bed.' She was so coldly furious, it was all she could do to speak, and her voice sounded deeply muted as it forced its way through clenched teeth.

'So you shall,' Laz intimated, turning her effortlessly round to face him. 'But not just yet.'

'Oh, for heaven's sake!' Rachel burst out emotively, her eyes flashing with anger. 'What is this? Another attempt to prove your superiority?'

He smiled, a wry, faintly cynical movement that wasn't matched by the expression in his eyes. 'I'm getting tired of your irrational behaviour.'

'Irrational!' she burst out, making an impotent attempt to wrestle free of him.

'By day a virtual virago,' Laz attested with

thinly veiled mockery. 'At night a willing
supplicant eager to taste every sensual delight.' He
stilled her struggling body with effortless ease. 'Oh
yes, my sweet wife,' he chided. 'Don't attempt to
deny it.'

The truth of his words was galling, and she felt
sick with the tumult of her own emotions. 'You're an
expert in the art of seduction,' she retaliated without
thought to the consequences. 'Why shouldn't I
derive pleasure from being in your bed?' Some
hellish imp prompted her further. 'After all, it's not
every woman who can boast such an honour.' She
knew she'd gone too far from the icy anger evident in
those stormy grey depths, and his expression became
incredibly bleak.

'You little fool,' he drawled in a dangerously
soft voice.

His hard intent stare created unwanted havoc,
and she stifled a silent scream as his grasp seemed
to bruise her bones.

'You're hurting me!'

'Believe you'll hurt a lot more by the time I
finished with you.' The chilling finality of his
words glavanised her into action as she lashed out
at him with her sandalled feet, fighting as if her
very life depended on escaping him.

Without any effort at all he lifted her over one
shoulder and carried her, wildly flailing, upstairs
to their bedroom, pausing long enough to kick the
door shut before crossing to the large bed and
dropping her unceremoniously down on to the
counterpane.

'You have precisely one minute to get out of
those clothes, or I'll remove them for you,' Laz
indicated with hateful cynicism. 'And I give no
assurance to treat them with care.'

'Or me,' Rachel blazed, and his eyes narrowed fractionally.

'You started this particular debacle,' he elucidated with brooding savagery, his hands going with slow unhurried movements to the buttons on his shirt, pulling it free from the waistband of his trousers, and when his fingers slid to the zip she burst into incredulous speech.

'What do you think you're doing?' Fear mirrored itself in her eyes, making them appear large stormy pools as he divested the rest of his clothes, and she was unable to tear her gaze away from the hard implacability evident in his expression.

'Don't,' she cried out involuntarily as he moved towards the bed, and sheer fright was responsible for the way she scrambled out of reach to stand petrified on the opposite side. 'There's an ugly word for what you intend doing,' she whispered shakily.

'Rape?' The query was lazily insolent. 'Oh no, Rachel,' he refuted mockingly. 'I won't give you the opportunity to defile me for an act of violation.' He moved slowly with pantherish grace, covering the distance between them with ease, reaching out to capture her as she would have fled to the door.

'Let me go!'

'Never,' Laz declared with irrevocable finality, lifting her easily into his arms and carrying her to the bed.

Rachel pummelled his sinewy shoulders, his ribs, and she gave an anguished cry as he began to remove her clothes within seconds of letting her slide to her feet.

'You barbaric fiend!' Disbelief widened her eyes

as he calmly wrenched the silk trousers to her feet, then followed them with the jacket and top, then the delicate scraps of silk and lace that served as pants and bra. 'You can't mean to go through with this!'

'No?' Dark eyes swept slowly over every inch of her, and she burned beneath his analytical appraisal.

'I hate you!' Scarcely had the words escaped her lips than his head descended, and she swayed beneath the bruising intensity as his mouth crushed hers in a kiss that was nothing less than a brutal invasion of her senses.

Stubborn determination ensured she gave no response as she deliberately became limp in his arms, forcing her body to remain still as his hands began an evocative path down the length of her spine.

He knew every sensual pleasure-pulse, and he played each like a virtuoso until fire ran through her veins and her whole body quivered with an emotion she was unable to control.

His mouth left hers and began to trail down the pulsing cord at her neck, seeking and finding the vunerable hollow at the base of her throat, then slipping lower to the full creamy breast and its rosy tip that positively ached for his touch.

An almost inaudible groan left her lips as his tongue teased and tantalised at leisure before trailing slowly to render a similar treatment to its twin.

'Damn you, Laz,' she whispered shakily, hating the slow ache that began deep inside and steadily spread to her loins, until her whole body radiated with an all-encompassing passion, demanding the release only his body could give.

She became aware of silken sheets beneath her back, the soft springiness of the bed, and she closed her eyes against the pulsing swirl of emotion as his mouth trailed at will over her body, tasting every inch as if it was an erotic morsel to be savoured.

Not content, he ignored her begging pleas, until at last he sought the heightened, throbbing core of her pleasure, and she threshed against his invasion, mindless in the throes of ecstasy and unaware of the faintly guttural cries that fell from her lips.

Then she did cry, slow silent tears slipping down each cheek as his mouth travelled up towards her breast, nurturing first one hardened peak, then the other, before finding her mouth in a low deep kiss that was strangely bittersweet.

If he intended to torment her, he succeeded, for never had she felt so tortured, *driven*, to a point where she became almost a crazed, demented being as she alternatively begged and pleaded for his possession.

At last he acceded, and the tiny animal sounds died in her throat as he led her with consummate skill to the very brink of ecstasy, pacing her pleasure with his own, until she clung to him unashamedly, uncaring of the tiny breathless kisses she rained over his face.

Nothing mattered any more. All the hurt, the pain, was forgotten as she luxuriated in their lovemaking, and it wasn't until she was on the edge of sleep that reality slowly surfaced, and with it came an immeasurable sense of despair.

Rachel woke late next morning to discover Laz had already left for the recording studio, and she rolled on to her stomach with an audible groan.

The memory of his lovemaking was a vivid

haunting entity, and closing her eyes didn't shut out the quality of his flagrant seduction, or her reaction.

One thing was sure, she couldn't remain in bed. *Bed.* It seemed to signify her downfall, and with an anguished groan she threw back the covers, reached for her robe, then crossed the room to pull back the drapes.

Standing at the window she stared sightlessly out over the beautifully landscaped grounds without really registering the neat borders, the trimmed shrubs planted with symmetrical precision at the edge of the long curved driveway.

Thoughts raced through her brain with kaleidoscopic confusion, each coloured segment seemingly symbolic with innumerable events that had taken place during the past six years. Assembling them into logical sequence appeared impossible, yet out of the chaos some reason was beginning to emerge.

Wasn't she attempting an encore of the first year of their marriage? Re-living the same insecurities, the same frustrations? Refusing to recognise that she'd changed, matured, *grown.*

Love was a gift. Unique—without, and beyond, price.

Six years ago she'd thought love could conquer all, and because it hadn't she'd stood back, separating the physical from the prosaic, refusing to let them merge, until they began to form two different entitites and she'd been unable to relate entirely to either. Like a child, she'd run away rather than stay and face the challenge of succeeding over difficult odds.

The knowledge rose like bitter gall in her throat.

Part of her warred against Laz for employing caveman tactics in enforcing a reconciliation.

Another part recognised the necessity. Perhaps when everything was considered, it had been the only way.

Rachel caught a movement out of the corner of her eye, her reverie broken at the sight of Prince and King, Laz's two Alsatians, gambolling on the lawn.

The house itself was perfection, its furnishings a natural complement to neutral-shaded carpets, the decor expensively elegant, but essentially liveable. Equally a home in which to entertain, or to aid relaxation. Somewhere she could live with ease.

A faint sigh left her lips. It would achieve nothing to ponder what the future would bring. One staggering fact was certain. Her life was irretrievably bound up with Laz, enmeshed to a frightening degree. Whether he chose to reside permanently in America, Australia, or commute between the two countries, she knew she'd go with him. This time there would be no running away, no further separation.

She felt the need to tell him, say with words what she knew her body cried out every time they made love together. Maybe tonight she wouldn't hesitate, hating herself as the slim wedge of courage slowly slipped to retreat until the moment was gone.

It was what he wanted, *deserved*, to hear. If anything, his loving became more exquisitely passionate with each passing night—almost as if he *knew*, and was prepared to wait it out until the last barrier in her mind had been removed.

CHAPTER TEN

RACHEL'S first week in Los Angeles set the pattern for the weeks remaining, and she filled her days shopping or sight-seeing. There were a succession of parties, dinners which Laz was expected to attend, and gradually these no longer represented such an ordeal.

As the night of Laz's final concert drew near, she became increasingly nervous, changing her mind a dozen times over what she would wear, and even now as she rode in the rear of the limousine *en route* to the auditorium, she was unsure whether the white gown she'd chosen was entirely suitable. Grecian in design, the bodice clung lovingly over her breasts leaving one shoulder bare, its skirt embracing her slender hips to fall in soft folds to her ankles. Her only jewellery was an exquisite diamond pendant on a slim gold chain, and a diamond stud in each earlobe.

Laz had gone on ahead with Mike in a separate vehicle, and despite his brief hard kiss minutes before leaving the house, she had sensed the tension evident, the build-up of nerves that precluded appearing live before a huge audience.

She'd wanted to say a few words, *anything*, to wish him well. Instead, she'd given him a tremulous smile and murmured something inconsequential that she couldn't even recollect within minutes of his departure.

Tomorrow they were due to leave for Hawaii.

Perhaps that was what they needed—time alone together without the countless interruptions from various people, each equally intent on encroaching on his time.

'Not long now.'

Rachel heard the quiet deep voice, and turned to the man seated at her side. 'No.' A professional bodyguard, hired specifically to accompany her for the evening. It was crazy—she couldn't even remember his name.

The limousine began to slow, joining the long row of Cadillacs, Rolls, which were permitted direct access to the main entrance enabling each to deposit their privileged passengers.

Tickets for the concert had sold out in one day, and now crowds lined the sweeping driveway, intent on catching a glimpse of the many Hollywood *names* who'd elected to attend.

Rachel felt the clutch of butterflies inside her stomach begin to beat their wings, heightening her nervous tension until she became almost paralytic with fear.

The sea of people beyond the tinted glass windows of the large vehicle was frightening, their avid fascination almost sickening as they pushed, screamed and fought to come close to the men and women they'd put high on a pedestal, admired and adored to a point of sheer fanaticism.

Security personnel flanked the entrance, and almost as soon as the car slid to a halt the door was opened and the bodyguard stepped out to stand waiting for her to emerge.

There was no room for hesitation, and Rachel took his proffered hand as she stood to her feet, then summoning a fixed smile she moved at his side, blinking at the constant flashing camera bulbs, more grateful than she could say when they reached the foyer itself.

There were ushers, trained dark-suited staff, who came forward to escort the famous to their respective seats, and the muted rumble of voices was all around them, becoming even more intense as they entered the auditorium itself.

'I'd like to see my husband.' Was that her voice? Had she actually said those words? Or was it a combination of her own imagination and wishful thinking?

How could Laz possess the courage to face all these people? Sing, perform, *give* so much of himself? What's more, do it with style, panache, while exuding an air of calm relaxation—even *enjoyment*.

'The show is due to start very soon.'

Rachel nodded. 'I know. Are you telling me it isn't possible?'

'Getting you back-stage will probably take five minutes,' her companion cautioned, and she drew in a deep breath.

'I'd like to try. Will you arrange it?'

Their usher was consulted, and after momentary hesitation he changed course and began threading his way towards the heavy curtains at one side of the centre stage.

Maybe she was mad, but she possessed a burning urge to see Laz, even if it was only for a minute before he went in front of the audience. A tiny bubble of hysterical laughter rose in her throat. God, she didn't even know *why*, much less what she was going to say! And Laz probably wouldn't welcome the distraction as he mentally psyched himself to go onstage.

Even as they retreated into the narrow hallway

and inevitable warren of corridors that existed behind any stage, the band's musicians were already filing through to take up their position.

It was a hive of activity, and Rachel's presence caused more than a glance of surprise in what was obviously a highly restricted area.

At last the usher paused outside a closed door, spoke to the two men outside, then Rachel watched as one of them gave a peremptory knock, exchanged words with someone inside, then with an indicative nod she was allowed to enter.

It was so much like something out of comic farce, it was hardly believable, and her eyes flew straight to the tall man standing mere feet away. She was unsure whether to smile or cry.

Mike was there, but after a quick glance he moved to the door, silently mouthing 'two minutes' over Rachel's head, then he was gone.

'Something wrong?' Laz queried, his gaze narrowing as he took in her pale features.

He looked dynamic, emanating a raw masculinity that made the breath catch in her throat. Attired in black hip-hugging trousers, a cream silk shirt, and a black jacket left carelessly open, he projected latent sensuality from every nerve and fibre.

'I wanted to wish you good luck,' she murmured unevenly, feeling she had to explain why, yet not sure how to proceed. 'There's a huge crowd out front.'

'So Mike tells me.'

If he was nervous, he covered it well, and she lifted a hand to smooth back a stray lock of hair, then let her fingers slip down to the fine chain at her neck, abstractly fingering its length.

'I'd better go,' she said at last, and took a few

steps towards the door, then she turned back as if motivated by some elusive celestial force. Her eyes seemed trapped by his, and she swallowed the sudden lump that had risen in her throat.

She couldn't move, and watched in mesmerised fascination as he reached out and caught hold of her hand, trembling as he pulled her towards him. Gently he lifted her hand, turning it upwards, then he buried his lips in her palm, opening his mouth as he traced an evocative circle with the tip of her tongue before drawing the soft skin gently into his mouth, teasing it with erotic sensitivity for a few heartstopping seconds.

His eyes never left hers for an instant, and when he released her she felt as if he'd made love, so intense were her emotions.

Whatever he was going to say was drowned out by the double staccato knock on the door. A slight grimace twisted his lips. 'Mike,' he acknowledged ruefully, his eyes darkening with regret, and she nodded silently, already moving towards the door, aware of him following immediately behind.

'I'll see you afterwards.' Almost as soon as the words left her lips she felt the brush of his mouth against the vulnerable hollow at the edge of her neck, and a shaft of pure pleasure shot through her body.

'It's going to be a long night,' Laz murmured with something like regret, and she could only echo his words. The party after the show at one of the elite restaurants for close friends and various associates would probably go on until dawn, ending with a traditional champagne breakfast.

Leaning forward, he opened the door and together they walked into the narrow hallway, then casting her a singularly warm smile he turned to the man standing beside Mike—the bodyguard who'd ridden with her, and instructed obliquely—'Look after her for me.'

Rachel watched Laz take a mouthful of Perrier water from the glass Mike handed him, then he was moving forward, his features set in concentration, his mind already focused on the moment he would set foot onstage.

Already the band had begun a prelude to the opening number, and she followed the usher, aware of the bodyguard walking behind her, all the way down to her seat at the edge of a centre row directly in front of the stage.

Laz followed one song after another, pausing in between to talk to the audience, making them feel they were a part of his act, skilfully injecting an incredible depth of feeling into the music so that his voice, his body, his entire soul appeared to be one pulsing heady composite that placed him in a class of his own.

The audience went wild at the beginning of each successive song, and Rachel sat in silence, mesmerised by his terrific energy drive, caught up with it to a degree whereby she seemed physically ensnared, sharing his emotions, feeling the tremendous drain, the inherent replenishing necessary with which to continue, until, after two and a half hours, he simply stood still in silence as the band played solo, then when there was no sound at all the crowd rose to their feet and began to cheer and chant, stamping their feet and clapping their hands as they asked for, demanded, a final encore.

At last the noise began to abate as they saw he meant to comply, and he signalled to the band, then turned back to the audience, his smile infinitely warm as he began to speak.

'I'd like to thank you all for coming tonight, for making this as special for me as I hope it has been for you. I'd like to introduce you to the lady in my life.' He moved to the edge of the stage, his hand outstretched. 'Rachel, come up here beside me.'

She didn't believe it, and sheer fright kept her firmly in her seat.

A roar went up, and after that there was no way she could refuse. Slowly she stood to her feet and walked to the nearest set of steps, grateful that he was there waiting, and she felt incredibly self-conscious, aware of the silent assessment of several thousand pairs of eyes as she took his hand and moved on to the stage.

The lights were almost blinding, their intense projection of electricity providing a slight heat, and she clutched hold of his hand in much the same manner a drowning man clings to a proffered lifeline.

He raised her hand to his lips, his eyes alive with deep slumbrous passion, and she gave a tremulous smile, silently begging him to let her go.

'The men responsible for providing such excellent instrumentals,' Laz continued, indicating and introducing them, one by one. 'My back-up singers.' Two girls and a young man came forward. Together they all took a bow, then quickly moved back out of the spotlights.

'And now,' Laz concluded, signalling the band. 'I'd like to finish with a song you're all familiar with—one I usually sing at the beginning of each concert, wherever I happen to be.'

Rachel heard the opening chords, felt his fingers thread themselves through hers, then his voice flowed softly, in French, and there couldn't have been a single person in the audience who wasn't held spellbound with mesmerised fascination.

When it was finally over, she moved with him to the rear of the stage, oblivious of the wildly ecstatic crowd. Through the maze of hallways, direct to the waiting limousine out back.

Hardly aware that Mike followed close behind, Rachel slid into the rear seat with Laz beside her, and when the large vehicle sped swiftly out towards the street she leaned back, enervated beyond belief.

'You're very quiet.'

She turned her head slightly and forced a smile to her lips. 'How can you give it all up?' she queried simply.

Laz was silent for a few timeless seconds, then he said slowly—'Nothing lasts forever in this business. Anyone who imagines it does, is a fool.'

'I know,' she acceded quietly, looking at him in the dim interior of the car, glimpsing the strength apparent, the cool unruffled composure. 'At thirty-eight, you still have ten, possibly fifteen, years ahead of you—on television, touring.'

'Maybe. But I wouldn't have you.'

The quietly-spoken words unnerved her. Somehow instead of giving reassurance, they had the opposite effect, making her wonder for the umpteenth time if she shouldn't have tried harder to understand his priorities, overlooked his incredibly taxing work schedule. Except then, five years had seemed forever, and deep down she'd harboured the doubt he would be able to keep his word.

She wanted to say she had been wrong in leaving him, horribly wrong; tell him how much she deeply regretted the loss of several years. Only the words wouldn't find voice and emerge from her throat.

*   *   *

Their flight to Hawaii was smooth and uneventful, and it was late afternoon by the time they reached their destination.

'It's beautiful,' Rachel accorded simply, slipping out from the passenger seat of the unpretentious sedan Laz had hired for the duration of their stay.

The bungalow stood on the edge of a grassy fringe just above an expanse of crisp honey-coloured sand that led down to the translucent blue-green waters of the ocean.

He'd said it was isolated, and it was—kilometres distant from the nearest resort, and not a soul within sight.

Laz moved round and opened the boot, extracted their luggage, then carried it on to the verandah.

'I'll bring the groceries,' she indicated, reaching for the numerous packages resting on the rear seat.

Within twenty minutes they'd unpacked the necessities, and Rachel looked around the spartan, but comfortably-furnished lounge.

The bungalow was small and strictly utilitarian, comprising a bedroom, bathroom and kitchen at the back, with the lounge running the full width at the front.

'Well, what do you think?'

She turned and gave him a laughing smile, her eyes sparkling alive as she answered. 'Marvellous. How long can we stay?'

'A week or two. More, if you want.' He crossed to stand within touching distance, his smile warm and incredibly intimate, and she wrinkled her nose at him.

'Don't leave the decision to me. I might choose—forever.'

'Eventually you'd crave reality. This,' he

gestured to the horizon beyond the wide expanse of sliding glass doors, 'is the stuff dreams are made of—at least, for me they are.'

Rachel felt her eyes widen slightly in comprehension. In all the times she'd cursed his lifestyle, she'd done so for the way it affected her. Not often had she considered how he viewed the constant interruptions, frustrations and irritations associated with his career. Reaching out, she slipped her arm through his and said quietly, 'Let's go and walk on the beach.'

One eyebrow quirked with humour as he glanced down at her. 'Shouldn't we change first?'

'Be a devil,' she taunted softly. 'Slip off your shoes and roll up your trousers.'

'Ah,' he mocked, touching the tip of her nose with a stray finger. 'I'm almost inclined to believe you're afraid to go into the bedroom with me.'

She looked at him in silence, her expressive features mirroring several fleeting emotions, then she offered gently—'Let's take it slow and easy—please.'

He traced the generous curves of her mouth, and his smile was strangely gentle. 'I didn't plan on doing it any other way.'

Rachel watched him turn and walk to the bedroom, to emerge within minutes attired in a loose cotton shirt and faded denim shorts.

Catching hold of her hand, he led the way down to the beach, and when they reached the hard damp sand bare inches from the water she broke free and began to run, catching her skirt up above her knees.

'Race you!' She turned and gave him a cheeky grin, then laughed as he began to chase her.

With his long easy strides he caught up with her before she'd gone more than a few metres, and she shrieked with fright as he grabbed her round the waist and lifted her high in mid-air to swing her round in a full circle.

'Put me down!' She was laughing with carefree exhilaration, and he grinned.

'Say—please.'

'Please.' She clutched hold of his hair for support, and with a deep tigerish chuckle he let her slide down to her feet in front of him.

'Hmn.' His grey eyes lightened and assumed a devilish twinkle. 'You look about sixteen.' His teeth showed white. 'Tousled hair, bare feet.'

'And you resemble a beachcomber.' She tipped her head to one side, considering him teasingly. 'Well—not quite. You're too well-groomed.'

'Give me a few days of no shaving, and you'll hardly recognise me.'

She pretended to shudder. 'Ugh!'

'Make up your mind which you prefer, wench. I can't be both.'

'I like you just the way you are now, today.'

His eyes darkened momentarily, then lightened as he smiled. 'That sort of remark is likely to get you kissed.'

She lifted her head. 'Are you going to?'

One eyebrow lifted quizzically. 'Do I need to ask?'

'No, of course not,' she answered quietly, part of her wanting to savour the gentle friendship they shared without compounding it with something deeper.

His hand lifted to tuck a stray lock of her hair behind an ear, then he cupped her face and brushed his lips against her temple.

It was a gentle evocative gesture that made no demands, and when he released her she felt strangely bereft.

Without a word he slid an arm about her waist, curving her close into his side, then together they walked slowly back towards the bungalow, pausing often as Rachel stopped to examine a shell, or Laz collected a pebble to send skimming out over the water's surface.

The following few days were idyllic as they fished, swam, despite cooler temperatures, walked along the foreshore, eating whenever they felt hungry, and after a leisurely evening stroll along the deserted beach they made love with gentle unhurried ease, then rose with the dawn to repeat the pattern all over again.

It was a reprieve from the pressures of an outside world, and they treated each ensuing day with infinite care, aware that eventually their idyll would have to end.

Television wasn't something they viewed very often, but towards the end of the second week a particularly blustery evening prevented their usual walk after dinner, and Rachel switched on the set, changing channels in an effort to find something interesting they could watch.

M.A.S.H. came up on the screen, and she crossed to the cushioned cane sofa. The episode was a particularly poignant one, and she became immersed in it without any effort at all. When the credits rolled she waited idly for the commercials to finish to see what would follow.

At the sound of the opening music Laz gave an imperceptible groan and rose to his feet.

'You can't want to watch this.'

Surprise caused a momentary frown until realisation dawned. 'It's an episode from your series, isn't it?' she queried slowly, not really needing confirmation as his image came on screen.

'I haven't seen it before'

His glance was sharp and far too perceptive. 'Not once?'

Somehow she couldn't quite meet his gaze. 'No.'

'In five years you were never sufficiently curious?'

'I worked several evenings a week,' Rachel revealed quietly. 'There wasn't much time for television.' It was nothing less than the truth. Impossible to admit that she'd studiously avoided the popular series because the pain of seeing him would have been unbearable.

Effecting a slight shrug Laz resumed his seat, and she fixed her attention on the screen with a mixture of emotions, aware that he was only acting out a part, but strangely caught up by intense fascination for something that had occupied a lot of his time and effort over the past few years.

After ten minutes she had to concede he possessed a natural talent, able to project the desired image without any seeming effort at all.

'You managed to kiss the girls,' she acknowledged with wry amusement, trying to suppress undeniable pangs of jealousy as he was portrayed in a clinch with a nubile brunette.

'Doesn't the hero always end up kissing the girls?' Laz alluded quizzically, and Rachel summoned a faint smile.

'And enjoying it, too, I'd say.' Lord, she sounded like a possessive child unable to share a favourite toy.

'It's essential to appear enthusiastic.'

'Of course.'

'Hey,' he chided gently. 'That particular actress is a very married lady. Her husband inhabited the set during the filming of that episode.' His smile widened and the corners of his eyes creased with humour. 'The instant the director called "cut", she'd switch off that sultry pose, collect her husband, and they'd closet themselves in her trailer until she was needed again.'

'I believe you.'

Laz lifted a hand to her hair, threading his fingers through its length in an oddly soothing gesture. 'You see what's projected on screen through the eyes of the camera,' he began quietly. 'The actors enact a scripted part. A slight smile lifted the edges of his mouth. 'It's difficult enough remembering your lines, following each pre-determined direction, hoping each scene won't run into more than five or six takes. You're supremely conscious of everyone off-camera—the crew, extras.'

Rachel knew what he meant from the few televised shows in which she'd performed choreo-graphic dance routines.

'Did you enjoy doing the series?' She was genuinely interested, and he gave a husky laugh, gently tugging her hair, pulling her inextricably close as he bent his head down to hers.

'*This* I enjoy,' he accorded musingly, caressing her mouth with his own, pressing butterfly kisses down the pulsing cord of her neck until he reached the hollows at the base of her throat, savouring that sensual, vulnerable spot with erotic deliberation.

A shaft of sweet pleasure exploded deep within, sending a lambent warmth coursing through her veins like quicksilver, and she let her hands slide up to link themselves behind his neck.

'Be serious,' she whispered shakily, experiencing a multitude of sensations as his hand slipped beneath her cotton shirt and captured her breast.

'I am,' he murmured emotively as his mouth hovered fractionally above hers. 'Very serious.'

'Laz——'

'No more talking,' he chided gently. 'I need to love you—over and over again. For all the bad times, the long empty years, until you only remember *now*.'

Her eyes grew wide and began to glisten with unshed tears, then she swallowed convulsively as he brushed his lips against the corner of first one eye, then the other, feeling them flicker closed beneath his touch, and his tongue edged over her lashes, tasting the teardrops gathering there, before trailing down to close over her mouth.

Every sensory nerve-end leapt with tingling awareness, making her whole body seem one large pulsing ache, craving fulfilment.

Deeper and deeper he drank from the inner sweet softness until his kiss became an exquisite ravishment that was nothing less than an erotic assault on all her senses, and she moaned an entreaty, begging him to ease the unbearable tumult of feeling he had managed to evoke.

Somehow her blouse was unbuttoned, her breasts bared and swollen, their delicate peaks signalling an invitation he had no intention to resist.

Slowly his mouth grazed an erotic path over each soft creamy mound, then settled hungrily over one erotically-aroused bud, taking it into his mouth with practised ease.

When at last he raised his head she was almost mindless, lost in an ecstasy so tumultuous she was incapable of uttering so much as a word.

He *knew*, his eyes deep and passion-filled, his own breathing unsteady. Without a word he gathered her into his arms and crossed to the bedroom, and his lovemaking seemed to take on a new dimension, almost a poignant sweetness, that made her want to cry for all the nights they'd lost.

CHAPTER ELEVEN

AFTER ten days in Hawaii they flew to Sydney, where they enjoyed a brief reunion with Mrs Devison and Rebecca, then connected with a plane to Coolangatta where they were met by the farm manager and driven south.

The forty-acre holding lay several kilometres west of Byron Bay, set on a gentle slope with wide sweeping views over hills to the distant ocean.

Rachel fell in love with the house, its solid brick structure blending beautifully against a backdrop of trees, and once inside she moved from room to room expressing her delight.

It was *home*, and it seemed to herald a new beginning, the foundations of which had been inextricably consolidated during their sojourn on Maui.

Settling in was no problem at all, and within weeks of arriving Laz called in tradesmen to build a studio on to the westerly side of the house.

Refurbishing took several weeks as they leafed through countless catalogues, commissioned the assistance of an interior decorator, then waited for the painters to finish, curtains to be hung, carpets laid, and lastly the furniture they'd ordered to be delivered.

At last everything was completed, and Rachel was unable to suppress an intense satisfaction over the restful blend of colours that seemed to flow through the entire house.

Predominantly a tasteful mixture of cream-textured walls, soft honey-coloured leather sofas and chairs, camel-beige carpets, and complemented by curtains and matching bedspreads in delicate florals.

There were only the finishing touches to add—ornaments, extra vases to hold some of the many blooms that grew in profusion outside the house.

Choosing a day when she knew Laz would be ensconced in the studio, Rachel collected the keys to the Volvo Turbo sedan, then drove into town.

A suspicion she'd harboured for the past few weeks required confirmation, and she wanted to be sure before imparting such precious information.

Almost two hours later Rachel floated out of the doctor's surgery, unable to disguise the sparkle of intense pleasure that lit her eyes. She felt as if she could smile at the entire world, and she probably did—well, everyone she passed on the way to the car.

The drive home seemed to take more time than usual, doubtless due to daydreaming over how she would acquaint Laz with the fact he was to be a father in seven months' time.

She'd prepare a special dinner. Set the table with exquisite china, crystal glasses, silverware. Candles, a floral centrepiece, fine wine. It would be perfect, and somewhere between the start and dessert she'd impart her news.

Ten minutes later she eased the car down the long curving driveway that led to the house, a slight frown creasing her brow as she glimpsed a late-model sedan parked beneath the leafy gum tree adjacent the garage.

To her knowledge they weren't expecting visitors, and she brought the Volvo to a halt, then hurried indoors.

There was no one in the lounge, and a faint

premonition niggled her brain as she moved towards the studio, her worst fears confirmed as she saw the man standing a short distance away from Laz, a glass held in his hand, his pleasant features carefully assembled into a warm smile.

'Hello, Rachel. You're looking well.'

'Mike,' she acknowledged a trifle warily before crossing to Laz's side, glad of the comforting strength of the arm he placed about her shoulders. 'How are you?' She longed to demand what he wanted, but a part of her already knew the answer. *Laz.* The question was where, and for how long.

'Mike arrived only a matter of minutes after you left,' Laz informed indolently, and she suppressed resentment that his visit had been carefully timed to coincide with her absence.

'You may as well tell me,' she said evenly, glancing from one to the other of them.

'Astute,' Mike acknowledged with a wry smile. 'Couldn't I be here for a purely social visit?'

'You could,' she agreed, shooting him a pertinent stare. 'But I doubt it.'

'There's a charity concert being held in New York,' Mike informed without preamble, his gaze startlingly direct. 'Several top artists have agreed to perform. Laz's presence would ensure the venue is packed to capacity.'

Rachel closed her eyes and swallowed, unaware of either action. 'When?'

'End of the month.'

Her head lifted fractionally, her gaze shifting as it caught and became trapped by those dark grey depths. 'Are you going?'

Laz's smile was without humour. 'I said I'd have to discuss it with you first.'

Her stomach sank, feeling as if it was impossibly

weighted. 'You want to, don't you?'

His eyes seemed to darken momentarily, then they became swiftly hooded as he effected a slight shrug. 'It's a worthy cause.'

Their brief idyll had been shattered. A few months, and it was starting all over again. Rachel wanted to fly at Mike in a rage, scream at him for not leaving them alone. Yet she did neither, moving instead to extricate herself from Laz's grasp, a polite rather fixed smile on her lips.

'You'll stay for dinner, Mike?'

'Thank you, but no.' He seemed genuinely regretful. 'I have a flight to catch back to Sydney in just over two hours. Another time, perhaps?'

'Of course.' So he was going, no doubt with the intention of leaving them to deal with the aftermath of his particular bombshell.

'You have a nice place here. Peaceful.'

Yes, she wanted to scream out. It is—*was*, until you came along to destroy it. 'Thank you. We both love its solitude.'

His gaze was steady, and did little to aid reassurance. 'I like Laz's new song.'

As a parting shot, it found its mark, although she did everything in her power to conceal the surprise it caused. Laz had been spending more and more time in the studio of late, but she knew better than to interrupt him there. *God*—so he *had* been working. Not merely practising, as she'd thought. What hurt the most was that he'd chosen not to tell her.

'We'll see you out to your car,' Laz indicated, moving forward with indolent grace. His actions seemed unconcerned, but his eyes were strangely watchful as they encompassed his wife's pale features.

Rachel moved automatically, feeling slightly numbed as she walked with Laz and Mike to the front door. At the base of the steps she paused, then bade Mike a polite farewell, watching as he slid in behind the wheel of his rented car, and it wasn't until he reached the end of the driveway that she attempted to speak.

'Why didn't you tell me?'

'About what, specifically?' Laz parried musingly, curving an arm about her waist as he turned back towards the house.

'The new song, Mike, the charity concert— anything,' she finished miserably. 'I'm a part of your life, yet there are times when I feel like a stranger.'

Without a word he swept an arm beneath her knees and lifted her high against his chest to carry her effortlessly indoors, straight down the hall to the large bedroom with its magnificent view out over the ocean.

Slowly he let her slide down to her feet in front of him, and linking his arms behind her waist he held her close as he lowered his head, his lips incredibly gentle as they brushed her temple.

'The new song was meant to be a surprise.' The words husked against her ear, and there was nothing she could do to stop the wild surge of emotion coursing through her veins as he trailed an evocative path along the edge of her jaw to the corner of her mouth.

'Mike is just as much friend as he is manager. I'd have been offended if I'd heard he was in Australia and he made no effort to get in touch.' His mouth hovered over hers, his tongue edging out to taste the gentle curve of her lower lip. 'The New York charity concert is something which captures my interest.' She felt his imperceptible shrug. 'What is a week of my time compared to the amount that can be raised at such an event?' His grasp tightened measurably as his hands moved to mould her close against his muscular length. 'As for you being a part of my life——' His mouth settled over hers with deep passionate warmth, and didn't lift for what seemed an age. 'You *are* my life. *All* of it, every waking, sleeping second of it.'

'When do you leave?'

His husky chuckle sounded deep in his chest. 'What a one-track mind you have. We haven't even discussed it. And it's *we*, as in both of us.'

She hesitated for a moment, wanting, *aching*, to tell him about the baby, yet unable to find the words. 'I don't want to go, Laz.'

'Hey, it's no big deal,' he murmured against the tip of her nose. 'We can make it as short or as long as we like. One week, two—or even stop off in Hawaii for a week or so.'

'I mean it,' Rachel affirmed steadily. 'I'll ring Mum and ask her to come and visit while you're away.'

His head lifted fractionally, and his eyes were dark and searching, narrowing as he glimpsed the resolute determination on her expressive features. 'It's both of us, or the trip is off.'

'Then don't go,' she blurted irrationally, pulling out of his grasp. Tell him why, a tiny voice prompted, but she took no heed. 'I have to fix dinner.'

'To hell with dinner,' Laz retorted with unaccustomed brusqueness. 'I thought we'd dispensed with each one of your misconceptions and numerous uncertainties once and for all—Lord, *months* ago.' He reached out and caught hold of her chin, tilting it upwards and raking her face with relentless scrutiny.

'Maybe I just shunted them into a convenient corner out of sight,' she murmured shakily.

'Rachel,' he groaned with exasperation. 'What the hell are we arguing about? You don't want to go to the States—all right, we won't go.'

'But Mike will be back trying to persuade you to appear somewhere else—if not this year, *next*.' Why was she becoming so neurotic about something that didn't really matter any more? A slightly hysterical laugh choked in her throat. She was just as much at a loss to understand her behaviour as he was.

'Composing, writing music is my forte, you know that,' Laz insisted hardily. 'You also know I consider our mutual happiness the most important thing in my life.'

'Let's just forget it,' Rachel begged, more sorry than she could say. 'I really do have to fix dinner. I've planned something special, and if I don't start soon we'll be eating late.'

Maybe he sensed her need to be alone, for he let her go, his expression faintly brooding as she turned and fled without a word.

In the kitchen she unpacked her purchases and stowed them in the pantry, placing those that needed to be kept cool into the refrigerator, then she hurried towards the bedroom to change.

Afterwards she could only be grateful for the number of domestic chores which kept her occupied right up until it was time to serve the evening meal.

Some kind of dogged persistance was responsible for keeping to her original plan in using the formal dining-room and utilising an elaborate table setting. She even changed into the new frock she'd bought the week before, unaware that the soft blue enhanced her skin, highlighted her dark blue eyes, and was a perfect foil for her hair.

Laz appeared in the kitchen as she was adding the finishing touches prior to transferring contents of saucepans into serving dishes, and he murmured appreciatively as he uncorked the wine, then helped her carry everything through to the dining-room.

It was when they were seated, their respective glasses partly filled, that he queried lightly——

'Shall I propose a toast to something specific?' His eyes crinkled with warm humour and one eyebrow lifted quizzically. 'Or did you simply feel inclined to put your culinary skills to the test?'

Tell him, a tiny voice prompted. But somehow the right words wouldn't emerge, and after an inner struggle she simply shrugged a reply. 'I enjoy cooking.'

'In that case—here's to a beautiful meal, cooked by my beautiful wife.'

He was humouring her, and it rankled. Effecting a slight mocking curtsy, she acknowledged, 'Thank you.'

They talked, meaningless conversational phrases that filled the steadily yawning void, and afterwards Laz helped her clear the table, dispensing innumerable dishes into the dishwasher while she scoured a large number of pots and pans. Coffee made, she carried it through to the lounge and placed both mugs down on to a small table between each cushioned-leather chair, then she took her seat, picking up a mug and holding it between both hands.

'Channel eight?' Laz had moved to stand beside

the television set, and was about to switch it on, his face turned towards her, and she nodded in silent acquiescence.

It was almost nine o'clock, and she felt strangely tired. Something she was beginning to notice increasingly often of late.

'Mind if I take this into the studio?' Coffee in hand, he stood regarding her, his expression seeming enigmatic, and she longed to cry out that she badly wanted his company. More. She needed his touch, his understanding.

'No, of course not.' She sounded so polite, it was almost comical. 'I'm only going to watch this programme, then I'll go to bed and read.'

His glance penetrated hers. 'Sure?'

'Positive.'

When he had gone she stared sightlessly at the screen, hardly noticing the constantly-moving coloured objects that were momentarily unidentifiable in her mind as she went over Mike's visit that afternoon.

Conversely, she had no more doubts or uncertainties. In that respect, Laz was wrong. If anything, her love was so strong, her belief in Laz, the man—her husband, so incredibly rock-solid, there could be no room for lack of faith.

It shouldn't be necessary to have to *prove* love. Either you loved to the nth degree, or you didn't. And if you did, that love encompassed everything. Hopes, aspirations, the passions of the mind as well as the flesh.

Laz belonged to millions through his music and talent. To fetter such a God-given gift was almost criminal. Mike was right. The charity concert needed the draw of top-line artists of Laz's calibre to ensure success.

Standing to her feet, Rachel crossed to switch off the television, then she resolutely made her way towards the studio.

If Laz was surprised by her appearance he gave no sign, merely paused from playing the guitar and shifted slightly on the high stool set close to the wide picture window whose view of the dark inkiness of merging sky and distant ocean provided a startling backdrop.

Closing the door carefully behind her, she crossed the room to stand within a few feet of him, and she linked her hands together in a gesture of sudden nervousness.

'The song you're working on,' she began hesitantly. 'Is it the one Mike heard this afternoon?'

'Uh-huh.'

Not exactly forthcoming, Rachel decided ruefully. 'Will you play it for me?'

His glance pierced hers. 'Now?'

'Yes, please.' It had to be almost finished, otherwise he would never have allowed Mike the privilege of a preview.

'The lyrics aren't complete.'

'It doesn't matter,' she dismissed evenly, and caught his slight smile.

'My toughest critic,' he vouchsafed wryly. 'And the lack of sufficient words don't matter?'

She felt astounded, and found it impossible to conceal. 'Tough? *Me*?'

'You.' There was a faint edge of mockery evident, and she glimpsed a brief insight to the inner reaches of his mind, amazed that insecurity could be part of it. Somehow the knowledge lent innate courage.

'Play it, Laz,' she bade gently, moving to stand beside the window, fixing her attention on the thin glow of moonlight shimmering the ocean's surface.

The introductory chords flowed with melodic surety, and his voice was both a cadence and caress. Even when the words came to a halt, the music whispered to completion without hesitation. It didn't take much imagination to appreciate what professional back-up could do to make it one of the best songs he'd ever written.

Long after the last chord was struck Rachel stood immobile, emotionally enmeshed by the spell of the music to the point of being oblivious to the slow trickling tears streaking her cheeks.

Slowly she turned to face him. 'It's beautiful,' she accorded simply, and began walking until she was within touching distance.

Laz didn't move, and she lifted her face slightly towards his, holding his gaze bravely.

The words she'd withheld for the past few hours came out easily, almost as if some inner voice was responsible for their fluid formation. 'I'm carrying our child, Laz, and its well-being is so precious to me, I can't put it at risk.' A faint smile tinged her features, and her eyes took on a deep glow. 'There'll be other times when I'll travel with you—along with our son, or daughter. Maybe both, eventually.' The smile widened and became vaguely impish, bewitching. 'I fully intend them to be aware their father is a very special man; to be as proud of him as I am.' She reached out and placed her fingers over his lips. 'So go to New York. I'll be waiting here when you get back.'

And she was. Watching the steady stream of passengers vacating the *Ansett* flight from Sydney at Coolangatta airport just seven days after Laz had boarded a similar Sydney-bound flight *en route* to the States.

At last he appeared, his height distinguishing him from most as he moved lithely across the tarmac to the Arrival lounge.

Rachel detached herself from the crowd, exulting in the way his eyes gleamed warmly at the sight of her, then she was in his arms, hugged close against him, and she raised her face to his, uncaring that their embrace was being witnessed by interested passers-by.

'It's good to see you,' she murmured minutes later when she was able to catch her breath.

'And you,' Laz husked deeply, and his eyes were alive with latent passion for an ageless few minutes before he caught her close against his side and began moving to collect his luggage.

'The car's out front. I'll drive if you like,' she offered, unlocking the boot. 'You can't have had much sleep.'

'I was able to snatch a few hours,' he responded easily, stowing both cases and an overnight bag, then he snapped down the lid and crossed to the front passenger seat.

Inside, he fastened the seatbelt, then stretched out his legs. 'Wake me when we get home, hmn?' A slow smile widened his generous mouth, and his eyes gleamed with ill-concealed devilry. 'Drive carefully, sweet Rachel.'

Leaving the airport terminal she sent the car towards the main highway, then safely on to the southbound lane, she picked up speed until she reached the designated limit, handling the large vehicle with ease.

The dusk of evening had rapidly darkened into night, and once clear of Tweed Heads, the street-lighting diminished, ensuring a need for total concentration. Bush-clad ground lay either side of the road, clearing now and then as they passed a number of small towns scattered along the coast.

Rachel felt the leashed power of the Volvo, and resisted the temptation to urge the speedometer even higher. Five minutes gain was nothing if it involved risk. Besides, there was a degree of pleasure in deliberately taking her time.

A faint smile parted her lips as the slow-burning warmth inside her stomach began to spread throughout her whole body until every nerve-end seemed vibrantly alive. Soon, very soon, they would be home.

Ten minutes later she turned in between the gates and eased the car towards the house. Without pausing, she activated the remote-control device for the garage doors, watching them tilt upwards with swift smooth precision.

Laz woke the instant she touched his arm, and he leaned forward to brush his lips against hers with a featherlight touch that made her ache for more, then he slid out from the car.

Indoors she hesitated in the hallway, turning slightly towards him. 'I'll make coffee.'

A faint husky laugh brought a faint tinge of colour to her cheeks, and she was powerless to prevent the deep thudding pulse-beat that throbbed with tell-tale rapidity at the base of her throat.

'After. If you must busy yourself with something, you can upack while I take a shower.'

Rachel preceded him along the hallway to their bedroom, and once there she set about sorting his clothes into drawers, putting a few aside to send to the drycleaners, and she had almost completed the task when he emerged from the bathroom.

With a towel hitched carelessly about his hips he

looked refreshed and so incredibly vital she was unable to take her eyes off him.

'I bought you something,' Laz slanted musingly, crossing to extract a slim velvet box from his overnight bag. 'Open it,' he bade gently as he placed it into her hand.

A ring, its gold band set with diamonds—expensive, ruinously so, Rachel suspected as he slid it on so that it rested above her wedding ring.

'It's exquisite,' she said simply. 'Thank you.'

'Thank *you*,' he husked solemnly, his eyes holding hers. 'For loving—believing in me.' He lifted her hand to his lips and kissed each finger in turn before letting his lips rest against the ring. 'This is for all the tomorrows—eternity.'

The prick of tears hurt her eyes, and she blinked to hold them back, too emotionally charged at that moment to even speak.

'Tell me how everything went,' she managed at last, and glimpsed the faint humour evident in his gaze. They'd spoken on the 'phone every day since he'd left.

'Later,' Laz accorded softly, gently pulling her into his arms, and an impish smile tugged the corners of her mouth.

'How much later?'

His arms curved round the back of her waist, bringing her close against the hard length of him, and his head lowered down to nuzzle the curve of her neck, tracing the softly throbbing vein with his lips, brushing back and forth until he felt the faint tremor in her throat, then he trailed a path to her mouth, kissing her with such infinite gentleness she groaned out loud.

Of their own volition her arms lifted to encircle his neck, and she arched her body closer, holding his head down to hers as she deepened the kiss, revelling in his response, and she gave a breathless laugh.

'I guess we don't get to have supper?'

His eyes were dark and slumbrous, heavy with passion. 'I have all I need—right here.' He kissed her hard, and she touched his lips.

'I love you,' she said tremulously. 'In every way there is.'

His hands gently dealt with buttons, the zip on her skirt, then finally the lacy wisp of her bra and pants. With incredible gentleness he laid her down on to the bed, and stood still, just looking at the beauty of her soft pale body.

Slowly she lifted her arms towards him, a sweet smile on her lips. 'Welcome home, Laz.'

Without a word he lay down close beside her, and slowly, gently, he trailed his lips over her skin, caressing, tasting, in an evocative journey of rediscovery that transcended to a wild sweet passion—consuming, exultant, and inviolate.

Coming Next Month in Harlequin Presents!

847 LION OF DARKNESS Melinda Cross
The New York doctor, who's helped so many cope with blindness in a sighted world, is baffled by his latest case—and a force that threatens the doctor–patient relationship.

848 THE ARROGANT LOVER Flora Kidd
A young widow distrusts the man who tries to come between her and her Scottish inheritance. He made love to her, then left without a word nine years ago. Why should she trust him now?

849 GIVE ME THIS NIGHT Vanessa James
Passion flares between a tour guide and a mystery writer on the Greek island of Paxos. But she's blundered into his life at the worst possible moment—because around him, she senses danger!

850 EXORCISM Penny Jordan
Once she naively assumed he'd marry her if they made love. Now he wants her to help him research his new book in the Caribbean. Why? To exorcise the past?

851 SLEEPING DESIRE Charlotte Lamb
After a year apart, can an estranged wife forget the solicitor's letters and the divorce proceedings? Easily—when the man she loves reawakens her desire.

852 THE DEVIL'S PRICE Carole Mortimer
The day she left him, their love turned to ashes. But a London singer is willing to bargain with the devil to be with her lover again—but not as his wife!

853 SOUTH SEAS AFFAIR Kay Thorpe
Against her better judgment, against all her values, a young woman allows herself to be drawn into a passionate affair with her father's archenemy!

854 SUN LORD'S WOMAN Violet Winspear
Fate, which seemed to have been so kind, deals a cruel blow to a young woman on her wedding night, and her husband's desert kingdom loses its dreamlike appeal.

Author **JOCELYN HALEY,**
also known by her fans as **SANDRA FIELD**
and **JAN MACLEAN,** now presents her
eighteenth compelling novel.

DREAM OF DARKNESS

With the help of the enigmatic Bryce Sanderson,
Kate MacIntyre begins her search for the meaning behind
the nightmare that has haunted her since childhood.
Together they will unlock the past and forge a future.

**Available at your favorite
retail outlet in NOVEMBER.**